SCARLET H

D0523713

Also by Danny Weston

The Piper
Mr Sparks
The Haunting of Jessop Rise

SCARECROW

DANNY WESTON

ANDERSEN PRESS • LONDON

First published in 2017 by
Andersen Press Limited
20 Vauxhall Bridge Road
London SW1V 2SA
www.andersenpress.co.uk

2 4 6 8 10 9 7 5 3 1

British Library Cataloguing in Publication Data available.

ISBN 978 1 78344 531 8

Typeset by Palimpsest Book Production Ltd, Falkirk, Stirlingshire

Printed and bound in Great Britain by Clays Limited,
Bungay, Suffolk, NR35 1ED

To whistle-blowers everywhere.
Keep up the good work.

PROLOGUE

The crows were already gathering, circling and flapping like evil black rags on the chill morning air.

Annie climbed out of the Land Rover and stood for a few moments, looking in at the field, imagining the freshly sown seeds just under the surface, taking their nutrients from the soil and, she hoped, already starting to grow. A cold wind came gusting at her, blowing her long black hair around her shoulders. She wished she'd stayed at home long enough for that second cup of coffee, but she knew that if she'd waited until Ken was up and about, he'd have begged her to allow him to help her. For some stubborn reason that she couldn't quite identify, it was important to her to do this on her own.

So she swung open the metal gate and then drove the Land Rover to the very centre of the field, a short distance from the old Carlin Stone – the big grey boulder that stuck up out of the ground like a giant egg of some prehistoric animal. Ken had once talked seriously about hiring a bulldozer and moving the stone, but Annie had forbidden him to touch it, thinking of all the old legends connected with it, the ones that her mother had told her as bedtime stories when she was a little girl. The sound of the engine scared up those birds that had already started pecking hopefully at the ploughed earth, sending them flapping and cawing into the air.

'You lads are in for a wee surprise,' she murmured, and smiled at the thought of what she had planned.

Then she went round to the back of the vehicle, opened the doors and started unloading heavy bales of straw, grunting with the effort. Next, she pulled out the wooden cross she'd already made, the one she was going to use to support her creation and, finally, she located the black bin bag of old clothing that she would use to form the body of her scarecrow.

She knew how to do it well enough. Her mother had always had the job of making the scarecrows for the farm when Annie was growing up and had taught her young daughter well. Annie's mother was known locally as a 'white witch', versed in the ways of Wiccan magic. The locals had thought of her as a healer, the first person they would contact when somebody was ill. Annie could remember how, every year, her mother had consecrated the freshly seeded ground with a spattering of bull's blood, an offering to the Cailleach, the goddess of the earth, in order to ensure a good harvest.

Those old ways were pretty much laughed at in this day and age, but Annie also knew that there were still some old crofters, living out in the wilds of the Highlands, who wouldn't dream of planting a crop without carrying out this ceremony first. Annie's mother had lived well into her seventies and swore that it was the same ritual that had kept her hale and hearty up till the very end. Sadly, that part of her mother's DNA clearly hadn't been passed on to Annie, but she felt she now had a very good reason to go back to the old ways.

The first thing she needed to do was to plant the wooden cross in the ground. She used a spade to dig out a narrow hole and then a sledgehammer to drive the thick vertical upright deep into the soft earth. By the time she had it firmly in position, she was sweating from the effort and also horribly aware of a dull pain, stabbing her deep in her stomach, her illness announcing its presence, reminding her that the pain she was experiencing was going to get a lot worse as time went on. The illness – it had a name but she absolutely refused to use it – would soon put her permanently into a sick bed, and not long after that, a coffin.

The specialist had found it very hard to break the news to her; he'd stared out of the window of his office the whole time he was talking, looking like he'd rather be anywhere else than there. But then, Annie in turn had the awful job of breaking the bad news to Ken and Rhona and that had been the toughest thing she'd ever had to do in her entire life.

Rhona had just stood there, staring at her mother in mute disbelief, and Ken – big, tough man that he was – had broken down and cried like a baby. She tried not to dwell on that, because doing so made her want to cry herself and she had already decided that shedding tears was a complete waste of time. It wouldn't change anything. No, she had to make herself hard inside and pretend that it wasn't getting to her, not for her own sake, but for her husband and daughter.

She laid the clothing out on the ground in the vague shape of a man – there was a ragged old tweed jacket

4

that had belonged to Ken's late father, a pair of tattered blue jeans, all gone at the knees, two battered brown work boots, the leather cracked and flaking with age. She had no idea who the broad-brimmed hat she'd found hanging in the cowshed might once have belonged to, but it seemed to her that a scarecrow had to wear *some* kind of a hat and she was pretty sure nobody was likely to lay claim to it. For the face, she had nothing more than a water-stained potato sack and, she told herself, she would have to make that work the best way she could. She glanced over her shoulder and noted that a line of crows was sitting on the wall watching her, as though waiting patiently for her to leave so they could resume their foraging. But Annie was having none of it. She wasn't going to see all her hard work destroyed by a flock of greedy birds.

She started stuffing the garments with straw, big handfuls of it, pushing and prodding it into position. She'd already tied off the legs of the trousers and the cuffs of the jacket with twine, as her mother had taught her, and the scarecrow's big figure quickly began to take shape. She'd brought along a darning needle and some strong thread with which she affixed the empty boots to the ends of the jeans. Likewise, she secured the hem of the jacket to the top of the jeans. A lot of farmers she knew used old gloves to form hands but she hadn't been able to find any spare ones. So she'd brought along a collection of thick dark twigs she'd picked out of the hedgerow and she pushed these into position in the straw-packed cuffs to form splayed fingers. They looked surprisingly convincing.

Now for the head, she thought, and she filled the old sack with straw, tying it off at the neck and tucking the loose folds of fabric inside the collar of the jacket, so that it stood straight up from the shoulders. She surveyed her handiwork for a moment and then decided that it was time to lift the scarecrow into position, up against his cross. She extended his arms out along the crossbar and tied them in place with lengths of twine. She straightened his boots so they stood flat upon the earth, and it really did look as though he was standing upright all by himself.

She took a step back and studied him thoughtfully. The rumpled old sack was nothing like a face, she decided, so she spent a bit of time, pushing and prodding it, making two indents for the eye sockets and another, deeper one for the mouth. Still not happy with her efforts, she crouched down, prodded her fingers into the mound of damp, freshly dug earth where she'd made a hole for the post and smeared some of it into the three openings, giving an impression of more depth. Now she reached into her pocket and pulled out the vial of bull's blood. In the olden days, of course, a bull would actually have been sacrificed to obtain the blood, a sharp knife drawn across its throat, but this small sample had been obtained with the help of the local vet who had used a syringe to extract what was needed and knew well enough not to ask what it was to be used for.

Annie uncapped the vial and splashed a little of the crimson fluid onto her fingers, then reached up to work it into the fabric around the edges of the scarecrow's mouth, just as her mother always had. She stepped back, looked again and decided, yes, he had features now, the various folds and creases of the sacking even seeming to indicate a misshapen smiling face.

Now for the rest of the ceremony. She took a few steps back from the scarecrow and gazed slowly around the field. She put her thumb half over the top of the vial and began to sprinkle the remaining blood as she recited the words that her mother had taught her when she was only little.

'By the power of blood
Make this corn grow strong!
By the power of blood
Watch over this land!
By the power of blood
Watch over this family!
Bind them and nurture them
And see they come to no harm.'

She splashed the last of the liquid over the smooth surface of the Carlin Stone and then slipped the empty vial back into her pocket. She stood for a moment, in deep concentration. She knew this wasn't going to change anything, but it had felt good going through the ritual, revisiting the days when she was little and didn't have a single care in the world. She remembered that there was one last detail that needed sorting out. She collected the hat and placed it carefully, almost ceremoniously, onto the scarecrow's head.

'There,' she said, and she felt surprisingly pleased with herself. She had made a very convincing scarecrow. Even Mother would have been impressed by her efforts. And now, what about a name? He looked like a . . .

Quite suddenly, it came to her out of nowhere. *Philbert.* She would call him Philbert. She had no idea where it had come from, it wasn't even a proper name, so far as she was aware, and yet . . . somehow, it really suited him.

'Pleased to meet you, Philbert,' she said, bowing her head to him. 'My name is Annie.'

He just stood there, looking down at her: a dead thing conjured from bits of old clothing and handfuls of straw. She felt vaguely foolish, but all the same she kept right on talking.

'I want you to guard this field with your life,' she told him, sternly. 'Do you understand?' She half turned and pointed to the row of crows ranged along the wall. 'Keep those lads out, whatever you do. And this corn . . .' She waved her hands to indicate the surface of the field. 'OK, I know you can't see it yet, but it *is* there and it's going to be here after I'm gone, maybe for years afterwards. It's your job to look after it . . .' She glanced awkwardly around, hoping that there was nobody within earshot to hear her words. 'And . . . Philbert, do me a favour, will you? Look after my husband and my daughter and anyone they care about . . . because . . . because I won't be able to . . .'

Quite suddenly the sadness welled up within her like a

great hot balloon, one that burst suddenly, filling her with a tide of bitter hopelessness and she was aware of her eyes stinging as the tears finally came. She hated herself for being so weak but she somehow couldn't stop herself and she was so angry . . . yes, sad too, of course, but the overwhelming feeling was one of anger, that this horrible illness could come along and take her away from her husband and her daughter and the farm they had made their home . . .

And the next thing she knew, she was hugging Philbert against her, pressing her face into his chest, her tears soaking into the tweed fabric of his jacket, as she told him about all the things she couldn't bring herself to tell Ken or Rhona – of the fear that gripped her every minute of every day, how she worried about how Rhona would cope and how Ken would manage to run the farm without her there to quietly push him in the right direction . . . it all came spilling out of her in a torrent and, once she'd started, she found that she just couldn't seem to stop . . .

When she had told Philbert about all her fears, the wave of sadness finally receded and she was able to get control of herself. She stepped back a little, reached out to straighten his lapels and tilted his hat to a rakish angle on his head.

She wiped her eyes on the sleeve of her coat and looked at him solemnly. 'I'm glad we had this little talk,' she said, quietly; and then laughed at the sheer ridiculousness of it.

She loaded the tools and what was left of the straw into the back of the Land Rover and drove back across the field, the vehicle bucking and lurching on the uneven surface. As she neared the gate, the crows flapped up from the wall, cawing raucously. They wheeled back and forth above the field and she could almost sense their confusion, afraid to go back to what they had been doing before because now a man stood guard in the middle of the field, watching them intently. Annie got out of the Land Rover and closed the gate behind her. The morning sun was breaking through the clouds to the east and, for a moment, Philbert was silhouetted against it, his arms splayed. At this distance, Annie thought, he could almost have passed for a real person.

'See you later,' she called and she even gave him a wave; but of course, he didn't respond. How could he? His arms were tied to the crossbar, and besides, he was only made of straw.

CHAPTER ONE

RUNAWAYS

Jack stared forlornly out of the car window. It was a pleasant June day, edging towards late afternoon and on every side, he saw nothing but hills and valleys and areas of dense coniferous forest – an unfamiliar landscape that stretched in all directions with no sign of a house or a shop.

He glanced at Dad, hunched behind the steering wheel. He was dressed in an old outdoor jacket and hadn't bothered shaving that morning, which was unusual. His jaw was covered with fresh stubble, his blue eyes fixed intently on the twisting ribbon of road unwinding ahead of them.

Occasionally, they drove past fields, enclosed by grey stone walls, the only sign that people actually lived out in this wilderness. Sometimes there were big shaggy orange cattle in the fields or the fluffy white bundles of sheep. Other times, it was just grass and dandelions or a crop of something that Jack couldn't identify. For a boy who normally lived in a city suburb, it was somewhat over-whelming.

He thought about his friends back in London who would already be missing him, wondering why he hadn't turned up at school that morning. Earlier today, they'd have sent him messages, asking if he was genuinely ill or just pulling a sickie. At lunchtime, they'd have mentioned him in their posts on Snapchat and Instagram, asking if anyone knew what had happened to him. They'd be home from school by now, ringing his mobile and getting no reply. It would seem to them as though he'd vanished into thin air; like he'd been abducted, which, when he thought about it, was pretty much what had happened. Of course, Jack had no way of verifying any of this, because he had been made to leave his phone back at the house in London.

The first that Jack had heard about this trip was the previous evening. He'd been settling down to play *Assassin's Creed* on his Xbox, when Dad had marched unceremoni-ously into his bedroom, not even bothering to knock. He'd gone out earlier for a drink with a friend from work and now he was back, looking harassed, Jack thought, his expression deadly serious.

'Pack some stuff,' he said. 'We're going on a trip.'

Jack looked up at him in surprise. 'What do you mean?' he asked.

'You heard. Just the two of us. It's about time we had a holiday.'

'A holiday, where?' he asked, baffled. This wasn't like Dad at all; he never did anything without serious planning for months beforehand.

'It's . . . a surprise,' said Dad. 'Yeah, I . . . thought you needed cheering up.'

Jack almost laughed at this. Dad was clearly the one who needed cheering up. Since Mum had run off with that guy from her work, he'd wandered around the house looking like he'd lost something important and couldn't remember where he'd put it. Jack hadn't really been surprised when the break-up happened, though. He'd seen it coming a long way off, even if Dad hadn't.

It wasn't such a big deal. It had happened to loads of Jack's friends at school. People moved on with their lives, that's what everyone said. Still, it had been a bit much when Mum made it clear she was happy to leave Jack with Dad until she'd 'sorted herself out'. Months had gone by and Mum had barely even bothered to get in touch, just the odd, awkward phone call and a card on his birthday, and that hurt. It made Jack feel that he couldn't really have meant very much to her in the first place, if she could dismiss him so easily. She was clearly having too much fun with her new partner to let some unruly fifteen-year-old get in the way.

It took him a while, but he had finally got used to the idea that he wasn't going to see very much of her. Oh well. He'd always got on better with Dad anyway. Mum was . . . difficult, always had been. Still, it would have been nice to be asked what he actually *wanted* to do. But he'd got to a point where he thought he had everything sorted out in his head. Now here was Dad, acting all weird, complicating things.

'When are we leaving?' asked Jack, apprehensively.

'Tomorrow morning,' said Dad, looking around the room as if trying to decide what things Jack should take with him.

'But . . . it's school tomorrow,' Jack reminded him.

Dad nodded briskly, as if to say, yes, he was aware of that.

'Well . . . you're not supposed to take holidays during term time.'

Dad grunted. 'I'll take care of it,' he said. 'I'll leave a message on the school's voicemail. We'll say you're sick.'

'Er . . . OK . . . well, what should I pack? I mean, how long are we going for? A night, the weekend, a week?'

'I don't know how long for,' Dad muttered. 'Just . . . fill a rucksack.'

Jack frowned. He didn't like the sound of this.

'Should I bring my laptop and stuff?'

'No!' Dad looked suddenly very agitated. 'Don't take anything like that. I mean it, Jack. Leave it all here. Your mobile, too.'

Jack actually laughed at this. 'You're kidding, right? Who doesn't take a phone with them? That would be . . . crazy.'

'Humour me,' said Dad. 'I want to . . . to see if we can manage without those things for a while.'

'But it doesn't make any sense. Dad, I'm not being funny but you're acting really weird.'

'No, I'm not, I'm just . . . I want to get away from all this for a while.' He waved a hand around at Jack's room. 'All this . . . *stuff.*'

Jack glared at Dad. He wanted to tell him that he liked 'stuff', always had. But Dad seemed really preoccupied.

He was pacing up and down, looking distracted. 'Dad, what's going on?'

Dad ignored the question. 'Pack your medication,' he said, as though he'd just remembered. 'You'll need that. Bring as much as you have, because I'm not sure when we'll be able to get to a doctor for a repeat prescription. And don't stay up too late playing on that thing.' He waved a hand at the Xbox. 'I want to get away early.'

Dad hadn't been kidding. He had shaken Jack awake in the small hours of the morning and, after grabbing a quick bowl of cereal, they'd left at first light, slipping out of the house, loading their stuff into the back of the Vectra and driving slowly away, Dad looking anxiously to left and right as he did so, as though he were some kind of criminal, as though he half expected the police to arrive at any moment and slap a set of handcuffs on him. Glancing back at the house, Jack got the craziest feeling that he would never see it again, but then he shrugged off the thought.

Of course they'd be back!

But then he looked at Dad's serious expression, his red-rimmed eyes, the thin lips twisted into a permanent scowl and he knew that something was very wrong here. But he couldn't ask about it. Not at first, anyway.

SCARECROW

The hours passed with painful slowness as they drove steadily northwards and still Dad hadn't told him what was going on. It was no good, Jack decided. It was time to ask some questions.

CHAPTER TWO
THE FIELD

'You want a travel sweet?' Jack got the tin from the glove compartment and offered it to Dad, but Dad shook his head, kept his gaze fixed on the road. They had been driving for hour after hour, mile after mile, stopping only once at a service area to fill the petrol tank and grab a couple of much-needed sandwiches. For some reason, Dad insisted on paying cash for everything, which was really strange. He usually slapped everything onto his credit card and settled up at the end of the month.

Jack was beginning to get very bored. He couldn't even play on his phone. He took a sweet for himself, slipped it into his mouth and returned the tin to its hiding place. He sucked noisily for a few moments and then spoke, for the first time in miles. 'So . . . it's somewhere in Scotland, right?'

'Hmm?' Dad appeared to have been lost in thought.

'Where we're headed? Scotland.'

Dad grunted, but didn't nod or shake his head.

'I mean, it must be. We passed signs for Edinburgh and Glasgow hours ago and we're heading north, so I'm guessing it's . . . like, somewhere in the Highlands?' He frowned. 'Only, we don't know anyone in Scotland, so . . .'

Dad sighed. 'It's near Pitlochry,' he said, as though that explained everything. He gestured to an ancient road atlas on the car's back seat, its pages splayed like the wings of the dead birds they kept passing on this remote stretch of road. 'You can have a look for it if you feel like being useful.'

'A *book*?' exclaimed Jack, in disbelief. 'I mean, that's a bit . . . Stone Age, isn't it? Why don't we just get onto Google Maps and . . .' He broke off, remembering. 'Oh right, we can't actually do that because some genius made us leave our phones behind, didn't they? Brilliant.' He reached back, picked up the atlas and swung it over onto his lap. He stared at the current double-page spread. 'How do I even . . .?'

'Turn to the back pages,' explained Dad. 'There's a glossary. Look up the word "Pitlochry" first. That'll give you a page reference. And then you need to find a village called Elladour.'

Jack smirked. 'Sounds like something out of *Lord of the Rings*,' he said. 'How do you spell this Pit-whatsit?'

'Pitlochry. P I T L . . .'

'Oh yeah, got it.' Jack turned the pages. 'Do you think there'll be a cinema there? Only there's a new film out on Friday I wanted to see. There's a bunch of people from school going.'

Dad shook his head. 'I'd be very surprised if there's a cinema,' he said. 'It's pretty remote where we're headed. That's kind of the point.' He made an effort to turn his head and give Jack an encouraging smile. 'Come on, it'll be fun. We'll be . . . going back to our roots.'

'Our roots are in Scotland?' exclaimed Jack. 'Since when?'

'Well, no, I didn't mean . . . our actual roots.' Dad shook his head. 'I'm just saying, we'll be going back to nature, won't we? Living simply and . . . naturally. Who needs computer games and TVs, anyway?'

'You're saying there's no TV?' said Jack grimly. 'Please tell me this is a bad dream and I'm going to wake up in a minute.'

'Well, I don't know. There *might* be one. I'm . . . not really sure.'

'What kind of a hotel is it that doesn't have a TV?' asked Jack.

'It's not a hotel. It's a lodge.'

'A what?'

'A lodge . . . it's like a small house. A cottage. Belongs to a friend.'

'What friend?'

'Douglas, if you must know.'

'What, Douglas from the bank? I thought he lived in London.'

'He does. But he has this weekend retreat.'

'Oh, so we *are* just going for the weekend, then?'

'I told you before. I'm not sure how long. God, Jack, you're so literal.'

They drove on in silence for a few moments while Jack studied his father, trying to fathom out what was wrong with him. 'You know we'll get into trouble, don't you?' he said at last. 'Having a holiday in term time and everything. You'll most likely get fined. That's what happened to Jonno's parents when they took him to Tenerife.'

'Well, that's up to the school, isn't it?' said Dad. 'Anyway, I left them a message. I said you were sick . . .'

'But that's not true, is it?' snapped Jack. 'And since when did you start lying to the school? You'd normally disapprove of it. I asked to take one sick day a couple of months ago, and you nearly had a fit!' He ran a hand through his long black hair. 'For God's sake, Dad, what is going on? Look, are you in some kind of trouble?'

'Trouble?' Dad looked alarmed. 'Don't be silly. Why would I be in trouble?'

'Well, *something's* wrong. You haven't . . . you haven't robbed that bank you work at? Are the police after you or something?'

'It's nothing like that,' said Dad. 'It's . . . complicated.'

'Well, look, you've got to tell me sooner or later. And I'm not a little kid any more, I can handle it, whatever it is. Only . . . we've driven hundreds of miles and you haven't told me *anything*. Not a word. And I need to know.'

Dad sighed. He glanced at Jack and then looked away again.

'I'll tell you tonight,' he said. 'Once we're there. When we've got ourselves settled in.'

Jack didn't like the sound of that. 'Settled in.' Like they were going to be there for ever.

'It's always the same,' he complained. 'You don't tell me anything. It's like you try to shield me from stuff, when there's no need. Like with you and Mum. I *knew* what was going on, the whole time. But you kept glossing over it.'

Dad looked uncomfortable. 'Well, if I did that, I must have thought it was for the best, mustn't I? I was trying to protect you.' He gave Jack a look. 'Hey, listen, did you take your meds this morning?'

Jack sighed wearily. 'Of course,' he said.

'Don't say, "of course". You have forgotten before, haven't you?'

Jack turned his head to look out of the passenger window. He'd been diagnosed two years ago. There was a name for what he had but he never used it. What it mostly meant was that he was prone to mood swings, shuttling between super positive and downright depressed. And when he was down, that could lead to negative thoughts. But the doctors had eventually found the right medication for him, something that smoothed out the rough edges of his life, so most of the time it didn't bother him too much. Oh, there'd been a couple of occasions, early on in the process, when he hadn't been prompt with his meds and when that happened, he was prone to having what the doctors called 'episodes' – seeing and hearing things that weren't actually there. But he hadn't had one of those for months now. Jack hated it when Dad made such a big thing of it. 'I'm fine,' he said. 'Really.'

'I hope so,' said Dad. 'After that fight you had . . .'

Jack sighed. The 'fight' had been no big deal really. A kid in Jack's class had somehow found out about his condition and had started making snide comments to his mates, about Jack needing to take 'weirdo pills'. A few punches had been exchanged. End of story, as far as Jack was concerned, but Dad didn't seem happy to leave it there. He wanted assurances that everything was OK.

They drove onwards into the wilderness. Jack tried to concentrate on the map in front of him but he hadn't slept much the night before and was aware of a grey fog hovering somewhere at the back of his head. He tried to shrug it off but its grip was powerful and he was dimly aware of it closing on him, tightening its hold. Dad was still talking, but his voice seemed to boom and echo, dissolving into meaningless fragments.

The map blurred and Jack drifted away.

He dreamed something weird.

He and Dad were still travelling but now they were walking, striding across a vast field of waist-high grass. A powerful wind gusted around them, making the grass ripple and sway, almost as though it was alive. Dad strode across the field, his gaze fixed intently on the way ahead, but it seemed to Jack there were things hidden within the grass, things that were watching the two travellers in silence as they went by. Jack kept looking this way and that, catching glimpses of movement, indefinable shapes that seemed to shrink back under cover whenever he attempted to focus on them. Then he came to one particular spot where a screen of grass appeared to hide a dark hollow and Jack slowed to a halt, because now he was sure that in the shadows of that hollow, something was crouched, something large and oddly shaped, waiting to spring out at him. Slowly, apprehensively, he reached out a hand to part the grass . . .

'Ah, there's the cross!'

Dad's voice cut rudely into the dream and Jack jerked abruptly awake again. It seemed to him that he had only been asleep for a few moments, but glancing blearily at his watch, he could see that more than an hour had slipped by since he'd first picked up the map. He looked at Dad, confused.

'The . . . cross?' he murmured.

'Yeah. Douglas said to look out for it.' Dad grinned at him. 'Great map reader you turned out to be,' he said.

'Sorry, I was tired . . .'

'Well, I suppose we *did* have an early start. Don't worry. I managed anyway. Got us here in one piece.'

Sure enough, the car was approaching a big stone cross at the side of the road, an ancient lichen-encrusted Celtic thing some ten feet in height, the three points at the top enclosed in a heavy circle. Carved into the base of the structure was what appeared to be a heap of human skulls. There were some objects standing on the flat base of the plinth on which the cross stood – a couple of odd-looking dolls made out of what could be straw. 'This place is going to be a laugh riot,' he muttered.

Dad ignored the remark. 'OK, so Douglas said the lodge is right beside a cornfield. We need to turn off straight after that.'

They drove on along the road for a few minutes, Dad studying the road to their right. 'I suppose this must be it,' he said.

Sure enough, the car was passing a small field, enclosed by low stone walls. Standing right in the middle of the field was a big, ugly scarecrow, his arms outstretched across a wooden frame. A wide-brimmed hat rested on his large head, but what drew Jack's attention, what really made him want to laugh out loud, was that sitting on the scarecrow's left shoulder was a big, black bird. Jack was just about to remark to Dad that the scarecrow was doing a pretty lousy job when something inexplicable happened. There was a sudden blur of movement – the scarecrow lifted a hand, grabbed the bird by the neck and pulled it towards his face. There was a brief commotion of feathers, a splash of something bright red and the bird was gone. A couple of black feathers trailed from the scarecrow's mouth.

All this Jack saw in the flash of an eye and then the car was cruising on, and Jack couldn't be sure that he'd actually seen anything real. He twisted in his seat to look back and saw the scarecrow silhouetted like a crucifixion against the reddening sky – but then the car turned off the main road onto a dirt track that led up to a small stone cottage. Jack faced front again, his mouth hanging open, telling himself he needed to take some more medication just as soon as he got inside.

Dad brought the car to a halt and sat for a moment looking at the cottage, trying, Jack thought, not to look disappointed.

CHAPTER THREE

CARLIN LODGE

It was a ramshackle, two-storey building that might once have been painted brilliant white, but had been weathered by years of rain and frost until it was an unpleasant shade of mottled grey, as though carved from a big slab of that pongy French cheese that Dad was so keen on. There was a wooden front door with a small glass window set into it and a slate-tiled porch, beside which an amateurishly painted sign announced the name of the place as 'Carlin Lodge'. A moss-encrusted stone lion stood sentry beside the door, its jaws set in a ferocious snarl. Jack and Dad sat looking at the place in silence for a moment. Then Dad reacted, his voice a little too loud, too chirpy.

'Wow, looks really cool, doesn't it? *Carlin* Lodge. I wonder what that means.' He looked at Jack as though expecting an answer, but when he didn't get one, he opened the car door and got out. 'Come on,' he urged Jack, 'let's have a look inside.' He hurried towards the cottage, fumbling in his pocket for the keys. Jack grabbed his rucksack from the back seat and reluctantly followed, but his mind was occupied with what he had just seen – or thought he had seen – in the field and it was hard to put the image out of his head.

The scarecrow ate the bird! The words were careening around his head in neon letters. *It ate the freakin' bird!*

Dad had found the key and pushed the door open. 'Ta-dah!' he said and they both stood on the step, looking inside. The door gave directly into a small front room. There was a shabby green fabric sofa to their left, and a scuffed-looking brown leather armchair. To their right there was a cast-iron fireplace with a small wood-burning stove squatting in a brick hearth. Further back was a battered-looking dining table with four chairs arranged around it. Beyond that, on the far wall, hung a mottled, fly-blown mirror, which reflected their own silhouettes back at them. The floor was tiled brick red and there was a dusty patterned rug at its centre. Jack noted with a sinking feeling that there was indeed no TV in the room.

Dad reached inside and flicked a switch, flooding the place with a dim glow that only made it look more desolate than before. Another switch turned on a faint porch light.

'Douglas hasn't been up here for a while,' said Dad. 'He thought we'd probably need to clean up a bit.' He glanced apologetically at Jack. 'It'll look loads better once we've put a duster around the place.'

Jack didn't say anything. He followed Dad into the room and looked despairingly about. There was no disguising the fact that the place was a dump.

'Oh, yes, we'll be fine,' said Dad, as though mostly trying to convince himself. 'We'll have a rare old time! You'll see!'

'Hey, at least there's a phone!' said Jack, pointing to a battered-looking black telephone standing on a narrow table in one corner.

'Yes, it's a landline, but we can't use it,' said Dad.

'Why not?'

'Douglas warned me not to,' said Dad. 'He said he wouldn't ring me on it either. If it *should* ring, we're to ignore it.'

'Uh . . . OK,' said Jack. 'Why, exactly?'

'Just being careful,' said Dad, mysteriously. 'Now, I wonder what's through here?' A door ahead of them led into a narrow hallway, from where a bare wooden staircase went up to the first floor. Further on, there was a tiny kitchen: a grubby sink under a window that looked out onto a small back garden, a pine kitchen table and four chairs, some battered worktops and wall cupboards. To their left there was a plain back door, which was securely bolted. Dad approached the sink and opened the cupboard beneath it, revealing a formidable array of cleaning products. There was also a large torch in there. Dad picked it up and pressed the button. A powerful beam shone out of it.

'What's that for?' asked Jack, suspiciously.

'For power cuts, I suppose. I believe there are quite a lot of them when you're out in the sticks.' Dad switched off the torch and put it back where he'd found it. He caught the look on Jack's face and tried to reassure him. 'We'll soon have this place looking spick and span!' he announced. He straightened up, opened a wall cupboard, revealing a few lonely-looking tins of food: baked beans, soup, macaroni cheese. He tried the kitchen tap and it made a strange gurgling sound before discharging a stream of brownish water into the sink. Dad put his fingers under the flow and frowned. 'There's supposed to be an immersion heater somewhere,' he said. 'We'll switch it on and then we'll have hot water.'

He looked at Jack again, as though expecting him to speak but Jack didn't really have anything to contribute to the conversation, so Dad led the way out to the staircase. He went up, his feet clomping on bare wood and Jack followed. There were two bedrooms upstairs, one at the back of the house, one at the front, with a tiny bathroom sandwiched between them. Both bedrooms were equipped with old fashioned metal beds, mahogany wardrobes and chests of drawers. 'Oh yes, this will be perfect,' announced Dad. 'Which room do you want?'

'I don't care,' said Jack bluntly.

'Well, why not this one?' suggested Dad, waving a hand around the front bedroom. He went to the window and gazed out. 'It's got the best view.'

Jack trailed sullenly after Dad and looked down onto the drive that led to the narrow road and beyond it, the cornfield. The light was fading fast but he could still make out the scarecrow standing in the middle of the field.

'I'll take the other room,' said Jack and turned quickly away.

Dad looked after him, puzzled. 'You OK?' he asked.

'Why wouldn't I be?'

'I dunno, you seem . . .'

34

'Confused?' Jack turned back to look at him. 'Well, why would that be, I wonder? I mean, you've dragged me out to this dump in the middle of nowhere that doesn't even have a telly, you haven't told me what we're doing here, how long we're staying . . .'

'I was going to say you seem worried,' Dad corrected him.

Jack grunted. He went out, along the narrow landing and into the other room. He dropped his rucksack onto the bed and sat down beside it, his arms crossed. Dad came after him, looking sheepish. 'You promised me an explanation,' said Jack.

'Er . . . yeah, I know I did, but . . . let's get some food sorted first, eh? I don't know about you, but I'm hungry.'

Jack nodded. 'I'm starving,' he said.

'Right. Well, there's supposed to be a village just a little way up the road. Why don't I go and get us something to eat, while you clean up a bit? You know, wipe down the table, sort out some cutlery . . . maybe put the kettle on?'

'OK.' Jack reached into his rucksack and took out his meds. He extracted a pill from the blister pack and slipped it into his mouth, then swallowed with well-practised ease.

Dad looked concerned. 'Isn't it a little early to—'

'I'm fine,' snapped Jack. 'Go and sort the food.'

Dad looked at Jack for a moment, then he went out of the room and down the stairs. Jack sat for a few moments, trying to evaluate how he felt. After a while, he told himself he was all right, but he still couldn't stop his thoughts returning to what he'd seen, or what he *thought* he'd seen, from the car as he passed the field. It was sheer nonsense of course, it couldn't possibly have happened. And yet, it had looked so real . . .

He shook his head, got up from the bed and followed Dad downstairs. He found him in the kitchen, filling a plastic bowl with cold water and washing-up liquid. He'd found a pack of J-Cloths in the cupboard under the sink. 'I've switched on the immersion,' he explained, 'but it'll take a while to heat up. You can always boil the kettle and add some hot water to this. Just wipe the table down for now and we'll have a proper go at it in the morning.'

'That'll be something to look forward to,' said Jack sourly.

'Don't be like that, it won't take us long.' Dad seemed to remember something. 'Douglas is coming up at the weekend and he's promised to bring us some proper provisions.'

'What *is* this place?' asked Jack.

'I told you. A weekend retreat. It was Douglas's grand-father's place back in the day. But the old man passed away a few years ago, and now Douglas uses it as a hunting lodge. Brings friends up here to do a bit of shooting.'

Jack raised his eyebrows. 'Shooting what?'

'I dunno. Grouse, I suppose. Pheasants. Stuff like that.' He indicated a tall wooden cabinet against one wall, which had a stout padlock securing it. 'That's the gun cupboard, I believe.'

'Seriously? He keeps *guns* in there? What kind of guns?'

'I don't know. Whatever you use to kill grouse, I suppose. Shotguns. I expect Douglas will show you them, if you ask him.'

'Weird.' Jack tried to imagine Douglas firing a gun, but somehow he couldn't quite picture it. He glanced at his watch. 'Hadn't you better get going?' he suggested. 'I don't suppose there's a twenty-four-hour Tesco in these parts.'

'Good point. You'll be OK for a while?'

'Sure. See if you can find a takeaway. I could murder a Chinese.'

'Well, I'll *look*,' said Dad. 'But I wouldn't get your hopes up.'

He turned and went out through the front room. 'Don't open the door to anyone but me,' he shouted, and then the door slammed shut. After a few moments, there was the noise of the engine starting up and the car reversing back to the road, then a deep, all-pervading silence. Jack frowned. He went to the sink, filled the kettle and switched it on; but even as he performed the action, he couldn't stop his mind returning to what he had seen in the field, and he knew that he wouldn't be able to leave it there.

In his mind's eye, the scene played over and over, like a clip on YouTube – the big black bird sitting happily on the scarecrow's shoulder, the right hand blurring as it reached up to grab at the bird's neck – and then the flapping, struggling shape of the crow being wrenched sideways and crammed into that big, open mouth . . .

Jack turned away with a gasp. It was no good. He had to know. He had to have a closer look.

CHAPTER FOUR
POKE

Jack crossed the road to the metal gate set in the stone wall and stood for a moment, gazing uncertainly into the field. The light was fading fast so if he was going to do this thing, he told himself, he couldn't afford to waste any more time. He certainly didn't fancy the idea of standing in the middle of the field in total darkness. It was then that he remembered the torch under the sink and he thought about going back for it, but decided no, he shouldn't need it. There was still enough light left and this wouldn't take very long.

The scarecrow stood gazing towards him, his tattered arms outstretched, his dark stick-fingers splayed. Jack examined the gate and saw that it had a simple latch with no lock, so he opened it and began to walk towards the scarecrow, kicking his way through the waist-high corn.

As he drew closer he realised that the notion of this thing being in some way alive was quite ridiculous. The effigy that stood before him, propped up on a crudely made wooden cross, was just a collection of old clothes stuffed with straw, which poked out in ragged clumps wherever the fabric of the garments was torn.

The scarecrow's face was made from nothing more than an old canvas sack, the features just folds and creases in the rotting fabric. All right, so two deep hollows *did* kind of suggest eye sockets and yes, there *was* something in each hollow that seemed to glitter with dark intelligence, but, Jack told himself, that would be nothing more than a couple of black buttons – and OK, yes, there *was* the moist line of a mouth that whoever had made the scarecrow had chosen to emphasise with red paint or lipstick. As Jack grew closer still, he saw that the chin was stained with a congealed red substance . . . and were those some small black feathers stuck in whatever the red stuff was?

Jack shook his head. That was stupid thinking, he told himself, the kind of thing that could easily set him off, and hadn't he come out here to convince himself that he'd been seeing things? So deciding that he was looking at feathers stuck in blood probably wasn't the best way to go with this. He shook his head again, harder this time, as if to cast off the notion.

Now he was standing right in front of the scarecrow and, because it was taller than him, he was obliged to tilt back his head so he could stare up into its face. He studied the indistinct features for a moment longer, assuring himself that, yes, it *was* just fabric, nothing more. The scarecrow was comprised of an old sack and some discarded clothing, the kind of thing that some farmer could have thrown together in half an hour. Nothing to worry about here . . .

Except that now he had the distinct conviction that the scarecrow was holding his pose, waiting impatiently for Jack to turn away so that it could snatch a breath or scratch its nose or perform a little jig . . .

'No,' said Jack, firmly, the way his therapist had advised him to, whenever he had doubts about something. There was a mantra he was supposed to say and he used it now. 'You're not real,' he said. He paused, then repeated it, louder this time, so there could be no doubting it. 'YOU'RE NOT REAL!' He felt much better for having said that and he turned away, telling himself that he'd go straight back to the kitchen and carry on with his cleaning duties.

He froze in his tracks. He had just heard something behind him, something that sounded like a slow breath being released. He whipped round again, aware of his heart thudding in his chest, but the scarecrow was exactly the same, the pose just as it had been before, the expression on the rumpled face identical . . . or . . . was it? Wasn't the red mouth curved into a bit more of a smile? Weren't the eyes that little bit wider? Jack let out a gasp.

No, no, no, he told himself, this was where he had to stop it once and for all, otherwise the notion would grow and grow and it wouldn't matter how many pills he took, he just wouldn't be able to stop himself believing that something was horribly wrong here. He knew only too well, he'd been in this position before. It was time for drastic measures. He took a step closer, lifted a hand and prodded the scarecrow in its chest. 'You're not real,' he said again and tried to tell himself that it *was* just straw under that jacket, even if it did feel more solid.

The canvas features stared blankly down at him and now it seemed to Jack that the smile was deepening, the corners of the mouth lifting slightly. Jack could feel panic clutching at him with cold fingers. 'I do not accept this,' he said, aloud. And for good measure, he stood up on tiptoe and bellowed into the scarecrow's face. 'YOU'RE JUST MY IMAGINATION!' Emboldened, he pulled back his right arm and threw a punch into its stomach.

Everything happened very quickly then. The scarecrow doubled over and from its red mouth emerged a harsh gasp of pain. The arms came down from the crossbar, the stick fingers groping at the spot where Jack's punch had connected. The face was suddenly, impossibly, animated; dark eyes blazed in those deep sockets. And from the open mouth issued a loud bellow of pure rage.

Jack stood for a moment, staring open-mouthed at what he had caused. Then fear started up in him like a burst of fire, flaring in his chest and sending waves of panic rippling through his entire body. Before he even knew what he was doing, he had turned and was fleeing across the field, as fast as his feet would carry him, kicking and stumbling through the corn, horribly aware of the sound of booming laughter from somewhere just behind him. He reached the gate in what seemed like seconds and vaulted over it, his trainers thudding on the tarmac road beyond. He sprinted towards the drive and along it, to the open door of the lodge and, as he did so, he heard a deep voice shout, 'Come back here! I want to talk to you!'

But then he was inside, he had slammed the door shut and he was crouched down beside the fireplace, fighting to control his ragged breathing and hoping against hope that Dad would be back soon.

CHAPTER FIVE
WHISTLE-BLOWER

Dad set the hot packages down on the kitchen table, wondering no doubt why Jack hadn't bothered cleaning it.

'I got lucky,' he said. 'There's a little chip shop in the village and they'd just opened for business. Lucky, because the general store was already closed.' He indicated the wrapped packages. 'I know you really wanted Chinese, but this is not so bad, eh?'

Jack nodded. He stood with his back against the kitchen wall, his arms crossed over his chest, telling himself that he was OK, that he'd just had one of his little episodes, all he needed to do was to ride it out, and before too long the meds would kick in and everything would go back to normal. It was because he was unsettled, he told himself, because he was in a strange place; he'd let things get to him, but he'd soon be his old self.

Dad was rooting in a drawer. He pulled out some cutlery

and wiped it down with the wet cloth, then ran it under the tap. 'I got you a chicken leg,' he said. 'I know you're not keen on fish. We'll eat them from the paper, shall we? And I picked up a couple of cans of Coke.'

Again Jack nodded and, when Dad indicated that he should take a seat at the table, he obeyed automatically, then sat there looking at the food as Dad put it down in front of him, as though trying to puzzle it out.

'Haven't had a proper chippie tea in ages,' continued Dad. 'These days, everybody says it's bad for you, but once in a while can't harm, eh?' He took a chip from his portion and pushed it into his mouth. 'Mmm, good,' he murmured. He stared at Jack, puzzled. 'I thought you said you were starving?'

Jack automatically lifted a couple of chips to his mouth and somewhere at the back of his mind, he registered that yes, he *was* hungry and yes, the chips *were* tasty and it would probably be a good idea to eat some more of them. He and Dad ate for a while in silence, but pretty soon it began to feel uncomfortable.

'So,' said Dad. 'I . . . promised you an explanation.'

Jack looked up in surprise. With everything that had just happened he'd momentarily forgotten about that. But now, he told himself, it would be good to hear Dad's explanation, if only to help take his mind off other things.

'All right,' he said. 'I'm listening.'

'OK, where to start?' Dad broke off a piece of battered fish and popped it into his mouth, then chewed for a few moments, the crispy batter crunching rhythmically as he ate. He took a deep breath. 'Jack,' he said, 'do you know what a whistle-blower is?'

Jack smiled. He couldn't help himself. The first image that sprang into his mind was of Dad, as a referee, sprinting onto a football pitch and blowing a whistle to announce that he was giving a free kick. But Jack knew this wasn't what people really meant by the term 'whistle-blower'. It was something a good deal more serious than that. There'd been that story all over the news, a few years back, and the same name still came up from time to time. They'd even gone and made a movie about him.

'You mean like Edward Snowden?' he murmured.

'Yes. Well, no, not as serious as *that*, obviously.' Dad gave an unconvincing snigger. 'But, in essence, yes, exactly like Edward Snowden.'

'Yeah, we talked about him in school. He worked for the CIA and found out that a lot of bad stuff was going down. And he lives in Russia now, because he'll be arrested if he ever goes back to America . . .' Jack broke off, puzzled. 'Dad, I'm not being funny or anything, but you work in a *bank*.'

Dad looked wounded. 'It's a pretty major bank, to be fair.'

'Yeah, but it's not like you're into secret spy stuff, is it?'

'How do you know?' snapped Dad. 'No offence, son, but you haven't the faintest idea what I do for a living. You've never shown any interest.'

'Yeah, but only because it's like . . . maths and stuff?'

'Well, OK, point taken. Maths *can* seem dull to some people. But never mind about all that.' Dad pushed a couple more chips into his mouth and chewed for a few moments before continuing. 'My role at the bank involves me working with shares. You know what shares are, I suppose?'

'Like when you buy shares in companies and that? And you can make money on them?'

'Right. So I work with this guy called Roger Ainsworth and he handles the portfolios of a lot of powerful people. I'm one of his assistants.'

'Oh yeah, Roger. He's the one who Mum always said

took all the credit for your hard work and left you with the crap to clear up.'

'Er . . . well . . . that's not . . .'

'She used to say if you had enough ambition, you could be doing his job, instead of running around behind him, clearing up his mess.'

Dad looked pained by the reference. 'Yeah, she may have said stuff like that from time to time. But . . .'

'All the time, actually! She used to say you were a mug to even let him get away with it.'

'Er . . . all right.' Dad waved a hand to indicate he didn't appreciate the interruption. 'Well, anyhow, a portfolio is just a name for a collection of shares owned by certain clients. And Roger was off on holiday last week and he asked me to handle some stuff while he was away. He let me have the passwords to access the accounts. He was quite specific about what I was allowed to look at, but . . . I was feeling a bit nosy, so I had a gander at some of the other stuff, while I was there . . . some of the high-level portfolios and, well, I happened to come across evidence of insider trading . . .'

'I don't know what that is,' Jack warned him.

'No, I appreciate that.' Dad frowned. 'It's highly illegal

– and the people that get away with it can make millions overnight.' He thought for a moment. 'I'll put it as simply as I can. The people that do insider trading are basically using tip-offs they've had from people working inside certain companies, to buy shares in their business just before they become really valuable, or to sell them just before they become worthless.'

Jack frowned. He thought he got the general idea, though it sounded incredibly boring, like it usually did when Dad started talking about his work.

'So . . . how many people were doing this?'

'Oh, a whole list of them! I had the evidence right there in front of me, so when Roger came back from holiday, I . . . told him what I'd found.'

'Right. And he was dead pleased with you, I suppose?'

Dad frowned. 'He didn't say very much. But he had that kind of look people have when they've been caught out on something. You know, that "hand in the cookie jar" kind of expression? He thanked me and said he'd pass the information on to somebody higher up. And I thought that would be the end of it . . . but, a couple of days later, I was called in to Hunniford's office.'

'Hunniford?'

'That's Giles Hunniford. The CEO.' Dad gave Jack a meaningful look.

'What's a . . .?"

'Chief Executive Officer. The big cheese, Jack, the head honcho, a man who wouldn't normally pass the time of day with somebody like me. So I knew something big was going down.'

Jack took a bite from his chicken leg and chewed methodically.

'And *he* was pleased with you?'

'No. That's just the problem.' Dad looked haunted by the memory. 'Quite the opposite, actually. He advised me to forget that I'd ever seen the evidence. Warned me that a lot of powerful people stood to lose money if word ever got out. People could even go to jail over it, he said. It occurred to me then that this went all the way to the top. He was . . . well, the only word I can use is, evasive. He told me to let it go, bury it . . . he even dropped a hint about a possible promotion coming up and how he thought I'd be the ideal candidate for the job.'

Jack grinned. 'So you told him where to stick it, right?'

Dad shook his head. Again, he looked disturbed. 'I wish I could tell you that I did. But honestly, Jack, I was thinking about that promotion. It was worth another ten grand a year and, well, there's the divorce coming up, everyone knows those things cost an arm and a leg . . .'

'Dad, you've always said that I should tell the truth at all times!'

'Yeah, I know I said that.' Dad looked embarrassed now. 'All I can say in my defence is, it's great to have principles but sometimes it's hard to stick to them.' He stared at his food for a few moments as though trying to puzzle out his own actions. 'Anyhow, I was all set to take Hunniford's advice and let the matter go.' He scowled. 'And then your mother posted on Facebook.'

Now Jack did a double take. 'Mum posted on Facebook? What's that got to do with anything?'

Dad was nearly squirming in his seat. 'It's just . . . well, she was going on about that new bloke of hers, saying how wonderful he was, how he'd flown her over to Paris for a romantic weekend . . . and how he'd organised a meal at some swish restaurant.' Dad's expression suggested that the food in his mouth had suddenly turned rotten.

'I can see that must have been tough,' said Jack. 'I think her new bloke's a bit loaded.'

'Tell me about it! He's minted.'

'OK, so it made you feel jealous . . .'

'It made me mad! Throwing his money around, playing the big shot. I bet he's got more than a few share portfolios, too.'

'Dad, you're not saying *his* name was on that list, are you?'

'Oh no, nothing like that . . . unfortunately.' Dad grinned wickedly. 'But, anyway, it kind of got to me, you know, and then I went for a pint with Douglas at lunchtime and I admit, I maybe had one drink too many, so when I got back to the office . . .' Dad paused, stared down at his food again, as though reluctant to continue.

'Go on,' Jack prompted him.

'Something just . . . came over me. I felt . . . I dunno, sort of . . . reckless. And I thought, "Damn it, why *should* I let this go? Why should I? These people are breaking the law!" So I . . . I did something really stupid.'

Jack leaned forward, intrigued now. 'What did you do?' he murmured.

'I leaked the list of names.'

'You . . . leaked it?'

'Yeah. I sent it to *The Guardian*. I sent it to the *Financial Times*. I sent it to a whole bunch of people in the media.

I did it anonymously, of course, used a dummy email address, but . . .'

'But what?'

'Well, I'm worried I wasn't as careful as I might have been if I was . . . you know, in my right frame of mind.'

'Not drunk, you mean.'

'I wasn't drunk, Jack! I'd had two . . . well, three pints of lager.'

'At lunchtime.'

Dad gave him a disapproving look. 'No need to rub it in,' he said. 'You're worse than your mother!'

'So, what exactly are you worried about?' Jack asked him.

'Well, obviously Roger is going to realise it was me. So will Hunniford, especially as I didn't turn up for work this morning. They'll know, even if they can't exactly prove anything.'

Jack paused to consider everything that Dad had told him. 'OK, so you haven't really done anything illegal, have you?'

'Haven't I?'

'No. You've told the truth about something bad that happened. Nobody can touch you for telling the truth, surely?'

Dad looked doubtful. 'That's just the problem. There are people who would tell you that Edward Snowden "only told the truth". And look what happened to him. He can't even come back to the country he was born in.'

'Oh, Christ, Dad, we won't have to go to Russia, will we? The weather's supposed to be awful there.'

That did it. Dad burst out laughing. Jack stared at him resentfully. 'It wasn't meant to be funny,' he complained.

'I know. But honestly . . . Russia? It's not going to be *that* bad! We'll just need to keep our heads down for a while. Until, you know, it all blows over.'

'Until *what* blows over?'

'Well, I spoke to Douglas last night over a drink, explained what I'd done. He seemed to think it was a big deal. A *very* big deal. He said I needed to make myself scarce . . .'

'Was that wise? Telling Douglas? I mean, he works for the bank too, right?'

'Yeah, but he's my best mate, Jack, we've been friends for years. And it was actually his idea for us to come here. He said that when news got out we'd be besieged by the media and . . .'

'And what?'

'Well, like I said, powerful people stand to lose a lot of money over this. They'll be looking for someone to blame.'

Jack pushed his half eaten meal away. 'Oh, that's great. You're saying we're like fugitives or something. You're saying that people are going to come after us.'

'Let's not get carried away.' Dad did his best to look confident. 'I'm sure it won't come to that. We're just going to keep a low profile for a while. It'll soon blow over. Douglas will be there on the ground; he'll be able to let me know when he thinks it's safe for me to show my face again.'

'Safe? Christ, Dad, what have you dropped us into?'

'Relax! Quit worrying. I'm just being extra careful, that's all. I'm sure we'll be fine. I thought we could, you know, use this as an opportunity to spend some quality time together. Just the two of us. Of course, I'll . . . almost certainly lose my job over this . . .'

'Your job?' Jack couldn't believe that Dad was talking about it so calmly. 'Wait a minute. They'll sack you because you dished the dirt on some bad guys?'

'Yes, but unfortunately the bad guys include the people who are employing me.' Dad shrugged. 'I hate the work anyway. I've hated it for years, if you want to know the truth. It's time I started looking for something else. Something . . . better.' He pushed Jack's plate closer to him. 'Come on,' he said, 'you need to eat more than that. All you've had today is some cornflakes and a sandwich.'

Jack sighed but he picked up his fork and crammed a few more chips into his mouth. Now they seemed to taste of nothing. 'But what are we supposed to do out here?' he asked through a mouthful of food. 'This place is like . . . the back end of nowhere. It's a wilderness.'

'Oh, we'll explore . . . we'll go for long walks. It's actually really beautiful here, Jack, there's all kinds of things we never get to see in the city.'

You can say that again, thought Jack, but knew he couldn't say anything about what he had seen in the cornfield earlier.

'You'll see,' said Dad. 'We'll get a good night's kip and everything will look better in the morning.'

CHAPTER SIX

NIGHT WALK

Jack lay on his back in the unfamiliar bed, staring up at the ceiling. The moonlight, creeping in through a gap in the curtains, threw strange restless patterns on the white plaster. He had been lying there for hours and his mind was a seething jumble of thoughts and worries and fears.

He tried to go through it all calmly and logically, in the hope that he would be able to come to terms with it. OK, so basically, here were the facts.

Number one: Dad had dished the dirt on a bunch of powerful people who would probably want to get even with him when they found out what he had done. So, no great worry there . . .

Number two: Dad had almost certainly lost his job. So once his meagre savings ran out, there'd be no money coming in. Great.

Number three: he had more or less abducted Jack and

run away to the back end of nowhere, a place where there was absolutely nothing to do.

Number four: he'd decided it was a good idea to leave their phones behind.

Oh, and *number five*: there just happened to be a talking scarecrow in a nearby field that ate birds and reacted violently when you punched it in the stomach.

Jack kept coming back to the last one, reminding himself that this bit wasn't actually real, that it was just a reaction to all the other stuff that had happened to him lately. Mind you, he had to admit that it was a lot more extreme than the things he'd imagined in the past. They had been fleeting, insubstantial things – whispering voices, the smell of burnt toast, vague lights and odd colours drifting in the air around him . . . and one time, out of the corner of his eye, he thought he'd glimpsed one of the hooded assassins from his favourite video game lurking in a corner of his bedroom, watching him. He'd only seen it for an instant, and when he'd looked again, there'd been nothing there. But it had freaked him out.

The scarecrow thing? That was too weird. There'd been so much detail. Too much for comfort.

He suddenly felt parched and wished he'd thought to

bring a glass of water up to bed with him. He lay there for a few minutes, trying to put the idea out of his head, but the conviction that he needed a drink grew stronger and stronger until it seemed like he'd never be able to sleep unless he had one and, eventually, he had no other option but to get up and go out onto the landing.

He stood for a minute, listening. He could hear the soft sound of his dad's regular breathing coming through his half open bedroom door as he made his way cautiously down the stairs, not bothering to switch on the landing light, not wanting to disturb Dad. The kitchen window gave him a view of the moonlit back garden, a few stunted trees and shrubs stirring restlessly in a gentle breeze. Jack switched on the light and the view was suddenly gone, replaced by his own reflection. He filled a glass at the sink and took a long, leisurely gulp, then stopped and stared at his reflection in the kitchen window, seeing a skinny boy with tousled black hair, looking anxiously back at himself as though he had the weight of the world on his shoulders.

And then, quite suddenly, he became aware of something else . . . something that he couldn't quite explain. He had the powerful impression that somebody was watching him. He continued to stare at his reflection and, an instant later, he thought he detected a slight movement out in the garden. Whatever it was, it was too close to be the trees he'd glimpsed earlier; this was something that he thought was just on the other side of the glass, only inches away from him.

A cold thrill of fear jolted through him, making his blood slow in his veins. He frowned, snatched a breath, and began to back slowly away from the window, aiming for the light switch beside the door on the far side of the room. It seemed ages before he got to it and, when he did, he reached out his free hand to flick it off. The kitchen was plunged suddenly into darkness and now he could see, quite clearly, that there was a face pressed up against the window.

The ugly crumpled features under the brim of the big hat creased into a look of baffled surprise at the unexpected absence of light. Then the scarecrow twisted away and was gone. Jack stood there, his heart hammering in his chest, the half filled glass of water still clutched in his shaking right hand, raining drops onto the tiled floor. He remembered to breathe and was about to yell for Dad but, at the last moment, something stopped him; the thought that Dad would come down here and he'd go to look out of the window and there would be nothing for him to see, just like all the other times that Jack had experienced 'visions'. And Dad would be perfectly nice about it – of course he would, he was never nasty in those situations – but nevertheless, he'd be worried and surely that was the very last thing he needed right now. No, thought Jack, not this time. He needed to try to make sense of it himself.

So he turned and went into the hall and up the stairs to his room. Once there, he climbed back into bed and pulled the covers up over his face, telling himself repeatedly that this was getting out of hand, that he needed to put it out of his mind and get some sleep. Fact: scarecrows can't walk and talk, they are just effigies made by stuffing handfuls of straw into old clothes. They are inanimate matter. But he couldn't get that horrible crumpled face out of his mind's eye, the way it had reacted to the sudden absence of light. And the fact that, as it turned away from the window, its dark eyes had flashed with anger.

For Christ's sake, go to sleep, Jack told himself. Forget about what you think you saw and go to sleep! But he knew that wasn't going to happen, not until he resolved this matter once and for all. And there was only one way to do that. After fifteen minutes of lying there, hopelessly trying to rid his mind of a jumble of thoughts, he sat up and pushed aside the covers.

It was no use. He had to go and look again. He had to know more.

CHAPTER SEVEN
PHILBERT

Moments later, fully dressed and carrying the torch from under the kitchen sink, Jack pushed open the front door and stepped outside, leaving it on the latch. He stood for a moment in the glow of the porch light, looking cautiously around, shocked by how eerily silent it was out here. Back home, it was never really this quiet, there was always something – the murmur of traffic, the distant rattle of a train, the wail of a police siren, a soft murmur of conversation. Here the silence felt somehow oppressive.

He looked up and saw the full moon, a shimmering orb in the cloudless sky. Around it were more stars than he thought he had ever seen in his entire life. The sky was stupid with them, glittering like handfuls of diamonds scattered across black velvet. Jack shrugged his jacket tight around himself and, gathering his courage, he walked towards the cornfield. He stood for a moment by the gate, steeling himself, before switching on his torch and walking through the corn to the spot where the scarecrow stood. Or least *should* have stood, because he had only gone a short distance when he realised with a dull sense of shock that it was no longer there – just the crudely made wooden cross that had supported its shabby figure. The cross looked gaunt and decidedly sinister in the harsh battery-powered light.

He reached the cross and stood there examining it, looking for clues. A couple of lengths of knotted rope hung from the crossbeam, but that was all. He swung the torch beam around the field but saw nothing out of the ordinary, unless you counted a big, egg-shaped boulder, half hidden by the corn. Apart from that the field appeared to be completely empty. What was he supposed to do now? He had come out here to examine the scarecrow again, only to find that it wasn't on the cross, but he had the distinct feeling that it might come back again and Jack had to decide if he wanted to be here when that happened.

And then the decision was made for him as he caught a glimpse of movement away at the top of the field. It was out of range of the torch and he strained his eyes to look, dimly making out the far wall and a thick belt of forest beyond it. Something was emerging from the trees, a dark, shambling figure in a wide-brimmed hat. As Jack watched, rooted to the spot in dread, it clambered easily over the wall and started walking across the field back towards the cross, pausing occasionally to reach into the pocket of its jacket and lift something up to its mouth. Jack waited, teetering on the edge of panic, caught between the natural instinct to run and the powerful conviction that he needed to stand his ground and face up to the thing that scared him. Somehow, the latter notion won out. As the scarecrow moved closer, Jack lifted the torch.

The scarecrow's reaction was dramatic. It lifted a stick hand to shield its eyes, its mouth drawn down in a grimace of discomfort. Jack caught a vivid detail. Something protruded from the scarecrow's lips, something long and glistening that twisted and writhed. At first, Jack took this to be an earthworm but then he realised, with a twinge of revulsion, that it was actually the tail of a mouse. Now the scarecrow swallowed and the tail was sucked in like a strand of spaghetti. The scarecrow swallowed noisily and then that weird mouth lifted at the corners into a horrible grin. In the light of the torch, Jack could see now that there *were* stumps of teeth in there, yellowed and rotten.

'So, you've decided to come back have ye?' growled the scarecrow in what sounded to Jack like a harsh Scottish accent. 'Come to have another go at knocking me down, I suppose.'

Jack shook his head. 'N-no, I just . . . I just wanted to . . . hey, you, stay where you are!'

The scarecrow had taken another step forward. 'Why should I?' he snarled. 'This is *my* field, who said you could come into it? Who gave you permission?' He reached those stick fingers into the pocket of his tweed jacket and pulled out something that wriggled and twisted in his grasp. Jack saw that it was another mouse, held delicately by its tail. As Jack watched in silent revulsion, the scarecrow tilted back his head, opened his mouth and dropped the creature in. 'Happy days,' he said, his voice muffled. He began to chew, making a horrible crunching noise as he did so.

Jack couldn't help himself. 'That is disgusting,' he said.

The scarecrow gave him an irritated look and now the torchlight reflected in his deep-set eyes, which really were much more expressive than mere buttons.

'I'll thank you to keep your opinions to yourself,' he snarled. 'Do I go around criticising the way you eat?'

He seemed to recall something. 'What was that you had for your supper, anyway? It looked very odd.'

'It was chicken and chips,' said Jack, horrified that he'd been spied on. 'And who invited you to go looking in our kitchen window, anyway?'

'Keep your hair on, pal,' said the scarecrow. 'There's no law against looking in windows, is there? I'm a bit nosy, that's all. You'd be the same if you spent as much time on your own as I do. Was that your father, sitting with you, by the way?'

'Er . . . yes, it was.'

'He doesn't have a gun, does he?'

'A g-gun? No, why would he?'

'Well, the other one that stays here, the big noisy lad with the red face, *he* comes along with people who have guns and, between you and me, they are not that fussy about what they shoot at.' He indicated a ragged hole in the right shoulder of his jacket. 'One of them took a pot shot at me, not so long ago. It was all I could do not to react, I tell you that much! Took every bit of my willpower to stand my ground and keep quiet. I had a good mind to tear him limb from limb.'

'Oh, but . . . you wouldn't do that, would you?' asked Jack, nervously.

'Of course I would! I hate guns and I hate the people that use 'em. It was lucky for him that Ken came along just then and gave him a right good ticking off.'

'Ken?'

'The farmer who owns this field. He looks out for me, does Ken. Told that idiot if he shot at me again, he'd take the man's gun and stick it where the sun don't shine!' The scarecrow cackled gleefully, showing those rotten stumps of teeth. 'That's what saved him. Otherwise he'd be in wee pieces by now and the crows would be a-peckin' at him.' He lifted open the jacket, exposing his straw chest, and indicated where a sizeable hole in his shoulder had been plugged with wads of crumpled paper. 'Ken's daughter had to do a wee bit of emergency repair work on me afterwards. So if you've got any thoughts about picking up a gun . . . I'd think again, if I were you.' He took another step closer. 'Like I said, I hate guns. They make me feel really edgy.'

'Stop right there,' Jack warned him.

'Why? What do you suppose will happen if I don't?'

'Well, n-nothing. After all, you're imaginary.'

The scarecrow looked fascinated by this. 'Oh aye, you were saying something about that earlier. "You're not real," you said. I think that was the gist of it. What's that all about?'

Jack licked his lips. 'It's just that . . . well, you're a . . . p-product of my imagination,' he said. 'My therapist says so.'

'Is that a fact?' The scarecrow gave an unpleasant laugh. 'Well, your therapist can go and take a running jump – whatever a therapist is! What do you think of that? Your therapist can go and stick his head in a bucket of fresh cow dung.' He cackled, reached into his pocket again and fished out another rodent by its tail. 'Ye'll have to forgive me,' he said. 'They're a bit moreish, these wee fellers. Found a whole nest of them in the woods.' He held the mouse out at arm's length. 'I don't suppose ye'd like to try one?'

Jack shook his head. 'No way,' he said.

'I think, "No, thank you" would be a more polite response, but suit yourself. And you don't know what you're missing.' Again, he tilted back his head. The wriggling mouse was dropped into that cavernous mouth and Jack closed his eyes as the creature was noisily chomped into mush. When he opened his eyes again, he saw to his horror that the scarecrow had stepped right up close and was now glaring challengingly down at him. 'So, come on,' he said, irritably, 'I'm still waiting for an answer. Who are you and what's your business here?'

Jack felt a flash of irritation. 'What's it got to do with you?' he snapped.

The scarecrow put out a hand and grabbed the front of Jack's jacket, then lifted him bodily off his feet. 'I'll tell you what it's got to do with me,' he snarled and Jack got a blast of his mousey breath full in his face. 'My job is to keep unwanted creatures out of this field and for the moment at least, that includes you. Now, speak up! What's your name?'

'It's J-Jack,' gasped Jack, struggling to free himself.

'Jack who? Jack o'lantern? Jack of the Green?'

'Just Jack! Please, let me go, you're hurting me!'

The scarecrow grunted, but he released his grip, causing Jack to drop unceremoniously onto his backside in the corn. 'What's your business at the lodge?' he asked.

'We're just . . . visiting,' said Jack. 'Me and my dad. We don't mean any harm.'

The scarecrow seemed somewhat reassured by this. He pondered for a moment and then reached down and helped Jack back to his feet. He extended a sticklike hand to shake. 'I suppose I should introduce myself,' he said grudgingly. 'The name's Philbert.'

'Philbert?' Jack narrowed his eyes. 'What kind of a name is that?'

'The only one I go by,' said Philbert. 'It's what the farmer and his daughter call me, anyways. No idea where it came from. But I actually don't mind it. I quite like the way it rolls off the tongue. And who are you, when you're at home?'

'I told you, my name's—'

'Jack! Yes, yes, but who *are* ye? What's your game? What kind of a feller are ye? Friend or foe?'

The stick hand was still extended so Jack took a chance and reached out to take it, mostly because he wanted to see if this strange fantasy his mind had created could be felt as easily as it could be seen. Sure enough, the sticks didn't feel anything like he expected them to. They were warm and pliant and there was a sense of real power in their grip.

'Friend,' murmured Jack, hopefully. He let go and looked at his hand. 'This is so weird,' he muttered.

'What's weird?' asked Philbert.

'This,' said Jack, making an expansive gesture with his arms. 'All of this. I mean, I'm from London. We don't have talking scarecrows in London.'

'I'm sure you don't.' Philbert scowled. 'I get the impression I'm one of a kind. Haven't seen any others like me, anyways.'

'Does anyone else know you can talk?' he asked. 'And . . . move? Does Ken know?'

'Of course not! And neither does his daughter. That suits me. See, I was put here to do a job . . .'

'To scare birds,' said Jack, and Philbert snorted.

'That's only a wee part of it!' he insisted. 'I'm also here to look after this place and to keep an eye on Ken and his daughter, see they don't come to any harm. But they don't need to know anything about me. It's better if they don't.' He seemed to think for a moment. 'You're the only one who knows I'm anything out of the ordinary and it's sheer chance that you found out.' He fixed Jack with a stern look. 'So, listen . . . have you told anyone else about what you saw?'

'No, of course I haven't. They'd think I was having an episode.'

'A what?'

'Never mind. I haven't said a word.'

'Well, I'd be obliged if it could stay that way. To be honest, I'm usually pretty adept at keeping things hidden. With you, it was just a case of bad timing.'

'Oh, the bird, you mean?'

'Aye. The bird.' Philbert seemed to come to a decision.

He slumped down on the ground and sat there cross-legged. He looked up at Jack expectantly, so after a few moments' hesitation, Jack reluctantly followed suit, setting the torch down on the ground and keeping enough distance between himself and the scarecrow so that he could make a run for it if the creature came at him again. As he settled himself, he couldn't help but notice that something was moving in Philbert's jacket pocket. More mice, Jack supposed, and he tried not to grimace.

'You see,' said Philbert, 'I didn't ask for this job, but I got it anyway, and I carry it out to the best of my ability. Well, you have to take pride in your work, don't you? Most birds take the hint, but you always get one or two of the bigger lads who try to push things, show the others that they're not afraid. That's when I have to make an example of 'em.'

'By *eating* them?'

'Aye. Serves 'em right. Have you ever tried crow, by the way? A bit stringy, if I'm honest, but absolutely delicious once you get the taste for it.'

Jack shook his head. He felt slightly nauseated. 'I prefer my food cooked.'

'So you said that bird you were eating was . . . chicken,' said Philbert.

'Yes. *Cooked* chicken.'

'Hmm. Never tried that,' said Philbert wistfully. 'I believe Ken has some of those up at his place. Maybe I should go up there some time and . . . borrow one.'

'It'd be a lot nicer cooked,' Jack told him.

'I don't have time for such nonsense.' Philbert waved a hand as if to dismiss the subject. 'Now obviously,' he continued, 'I do most of my foraging at night, when there's nobody around to see me. That's only common sense. But then that bird came and sat on my shoulder in broad daylight. Bold as brass, he was, saying, "Look at me, look at me, I'm not afraid!"' He sneered. 'Stupid creature! Of course, I couldn't let that go. If word got around the other birds, they'd *all* be trying it on. So I had to react, didn't I? But just as I did, along came your car. And if there'd only been a driver, I'd still probably have been all right, because they do tend to keep their eyes on the road, right? But no, you were looking out of the window and I saw you react. And I thought, "Well, no worries, he'll be miles away by the time it registers with him," but no sooner had I thought that, then the car pulled in to the lodge and I said to myself, "Philbert, this could be awkward."'

He shook his head, scattering bits of straw in all directions. 'When you came back later on, I knew the game was up, but I could probably still have bluffed it out if I hadn't reacted when you punched me. Caught me completely by surprise, you did, so . . .' He rubbed his stomach with a stick hand. 'I may only be made of straw,' he said, 'but by golly it hurt!' He spread his hands in a gesture that said, *What can I do?* 'So now you know about me,' he said. 'Where do we go from here?'

Jack didn't know what to say to that. He had come out tonight to try and dispel the idea of a talking scarecrow. Now it had all got horribly complicated.

'Look,' he said. 'I don't know about any of this. When I've seen or heard stuff before, it's just been like . . . you know, glimpses . . . bits and pieces. But this . . . I don't know what this is about. This feels . . . real.'

'Eh? That's because I *am* real, you numpty.'

'But you can't be! You're . . . just some old clothes stuffed with straw.'

Philbert nodded. 'I take your point,' he said. 'And I agree, that's really all I ought to be. But somehow . . . I don't exactly know how, but I seem to have *blossomed* somewhat. Believe me, it's as confusing to me as it must be to you.

75

One minute, I didn't exist and the next . . . well, I just sort of blinked into existence and there I was, stood in this field, doing the job I'd been put here to do.'

'How long ago was that?' asked Jack.

'Well, now you're asking!' observed Philbert. 'How do I know how long ago it was? Ages, it seems like. There I was, tied to a post watching the world go by . . . and after a while, I realised that I was hungry and there were all these wee feathered parcels of tastiness flappin' all around me. Well, what's a feller to do? Survival, that's the name of the game.' He grinned at Jack, once again displaying those rotten teeth. 'So what about ye?' he asked.

'Me?'

'Aye, what brings you to this part of the world? From your voice, I can tell you're not a local. On holiday, I suppose. Planning on going rambling or canoeing or some such nonsense?'

'No,' said Jack. 'No, I'm not on holiday. I . . . my dad . . .'

'Aye?'

'I'm not even sure he'd want me to tell you about it.' Jack looked anxiously back towards the lodge. 'You know, I really should be getting back now. It's kind of late and if Dad wakes up and finds me out of bed . . .'

'I get the picture,' murmured Philbert. 'Well, listen, let's not be making a habit of this. You know about me now and I'd appreciate it if you just kept it to yourself. To be honest, I'm not a great one for company.'

'Then . . . why were you peering in the window?'

'Like I said, I'm nosy. Not a crime, is it? No, it's best you stay over there and I stay out here. If you should feel the need to talk to me again . . .'

'Yes?'

'Make sure it's at night. I don't want you setting foot in this field in broad daylight. Do I make myself clear?'

'Crystal,' said Jack. He got to his feet and picked up the torch. 'But . . . chances are I'll never see you again, anyway.'

'Now what makes you say that?' asked Philbert, standing up himself.

'Well, my medication could kick in at any minute and you'll just go back to being an ordinary scarecrow.'

'I wouldn't count on it,' said Philbert. 'I'm pretty sure I'm real. The last time I checked, I definitely was.' He rummaged in his pocket and pulled out another mouse. 'Last chance,' he said. 'Want to try one?'

Jack suppressed a shudder. 'No!' he said. 'No, thank you,'

he added, remembering his manners. He smiled. 'If I ever do come back . . .'

'Yes?'

'Maybe I'll bring you a chicken leg.'

Philbert grunted. 'Up to you,' he said.

'A cooked one from the chippie. Just to show you what you've been missing.'

'I prefer my meat raw,' said Philbert and he chomped eagerly down on his whiskered snack. 'And still alive, if possible.'

'Umm . . . well . . . er . . . I'll say goodnight then.'

'Aye. And listen to me. Don't go getting ideas. You're to tell nobody about me. Understand?'

'Sure. Whatever you say.'

'If I *do* find out you've been blabbing, there's nothing to stop me walking up to that place of yours and coming inside, one of these dark nights. Trust me, you do not want that to happen.'

Jack gulped, nodded. He walked back towards the lodge. When he reached the gate, he turned for another look. Philbert was standing back up against his cross, his arms extended. Jack lifted a hand to wave but got no reaction. This made him wonder, once again, if he hadn't imagined the whole thing. But, he told himself, real or imaginary, he needed to be careful. He wouldn't want to get on the wrong side of Philbert. He was too unpredictable.

Moments later, he was back in the lodge. He crept up to his room, undressed and slipped beneath the covers, which were still warm from before.

'I'm going barmy,' he murmured but found that, strangely, the thought didn't worry him in the least. He closed his eyes and was asleep in moments.

CHAPTER EIGHT
THE VISIT

Jack woke to the appetising smell of frying bacon. It made his stomach rumble. He lay in bed for a while, looking around at the unfamiliar room, piecing together the events of the previous night and trying to convince himself that it had all been some incredibly detailed dream. But it wasn't easy. If it *had* been a dream, it was like none he had ever experienced in his entire life before. He remembered the image of the mouse's tail sticking out from between Philbert's lips and felt faintly nauseous. Philbert, he thought. Where did that name come from?

The smell of bacon was becoming more intense so, after a few more minutes, Jack got up and, still dressed in his pyjamas, he wandered out onto the landing. Dad's bedroom door was open and Jack saw that the room was empty so he walked over to the window to look out across the cornfield. He was perturbed to see that, once again,

Philbert wasn't there; only the rough wooden cross, jutting up starkly in the midst of the corn. And that worried Jack. Hadn't Philbert told him, just last night, that he only ever left his post under the cover of darkness? So where was he now?

Jack frowned. He could hear Dad moving about in the kitchen and talking to somebody. Douglas, Jack assumed; though, wasn't he supposed to be coming some time tomorrow? Why the change of plan? Jack went downstairs and looked along the hallway to the kitchen. There was Dad, standing at the stove and chatting away to somebody who must have been seated at the pine table, somebody who for the moment was hidden from Jack's view by the half open door. As he approached the kitchen, Dad looked up and smiled.

'Oh, so you're awake at last, are you?' he said. 'I was just thinking about giving you a shout. Fancy a fry up?' Jack nodded eagerly and stepped into the kitchen. 'We have a guest this morning,' added Dad, nodding towards the table. 'Say hello.' Jack turned, smiling, fully expecting to see Douglas, but he nearly fell down in shock when he registered that it was actually Philbert sitting at the table, grinning eerily, a knife and fork clutched in his stick hands.

Jack said something short and sharp. He wasn't sure exactly what he said but Dad clearly didn't like it.

'Hey, you, mind your language!' he complained. 'Do you want a fried egg?'

Jack turned back to look at Dad, feeling the panic hammering through him. 'Dad, wh-what's going on?' he cried.

Dad ignored the question. He was holding an egg over the frying pan, where rashers of bacon already hissed and sputtered. Dad cracked the egg on the edge of the pan and pulled the shell apart. A weird creature fluttered out – a mouse with crow's wings. It started to flap excitedly around the kitchen. Then there was a loud crash as the table tipped over, scattering cups and plates in all directions and Jack turned to see that Philbert had leaped up from his seat and was now chasing the mouse around the room, his arms extended, his claw-like hands ready to grab it and stuff it into his mouth.

'Now, that's what I call a bad egg,' said Dad, cheerfully.

Jack opened his eyes with a gasp and sat up in bed, his face drenched with sweat. There was no smell of bacon, this time. He sat for a minute, letting his breathing settle back to something like normal, telling himself that everything was all right, he'd been dreaming again and maybe it had just been a continuation of the detailed dream he'd had earlier, the one where he'd gone into the cornfield and talked to the scarecrow. He threw back the duvet, jumped up and went straight out onto the landing. Just as before, Dad's bedroom door was open but Jack could see that, this time, he was still fast asleep in his bed, the covers up over his head. Jack walked quietly past him, went to the window and eased back the curtain. He was very relieved to see that Philbert was in his customary position in the centre of the field, arms stretched against his cross. Jack let out a long slow breath.

But his relief was short lived because now he heard the sound of an engine approaching the house and, a few moments later, a muddy red tractor rumbled along the narrow drive and pulled to a halt alongside the Vectra. A thick-set man dressed in a waterproof jacket and a red baseball cap sat in the driver's seat and, standing beside him, hanging onto the side of the cab, was a skinny girl wearing navy blue overalls.

Jack remembered that Philbert had said something about the farmer having a daughter, which made him think that last night couldn't have been a dream, after all, or how else would he have known about her? Her shoulder-length hair was red, almost ginger, and Jack could see that the overalls were several sizes too big for her, cinched tight at the waist with a big leather belt. As the tractor came to a halt, she glanced up at the window and her mouth curved into a smile as she saw Jack looking down at her. He stepped instinctively back, letting the curtain fall over the window.

'Dad!' he said, urgently. 'Dad, wake up, we've got visitors!'

Dad stirred, groaned, and raised himself into a sitting position. He looked suddenly anxious. 'Visitors?' he murmured. 'What sort of visitors?'

'I don't know. I guess it's the farmer and his daughter, they're on a red tractor.'

Dad visibly relaxed. 'A tractor? Oh yeah, you're right, it'll just be the local farmer,' he said, pushing aside the covers and reaching for his jeans. 'Douglas said he'd most likely call. He keeps an eye on the place. We'll just pretend there's nobody home.'

Jack shook his head. 'I think they already saw me at the window.'

Just then the doorbell shrilled, making Jack start.

Dad sighed. 'OK, I'm sure it'll be all right. We'll get rid

of them as quickly as possible. Do me a favour, will you? Go down and open the door.'

'But I'm still in my pyjamas!'

'Oh, you'll be fine. This is the countryside, they're more relaxed about that kind of stuff here. Go on, I'll be down in a sec.'

Jack went down and reluctantly opened the door to reveal the two strangers standing on the doorstep. The man, a big ruddy-faced fellow, smiled and extended a hand. 'Good morning,' he said, speaking with a pronounced Scottish accent. 'Ken McFarlane, from the farm up the road.'

Jack didn't say anything. *Ken. Philbert said last night that was the farmer's name!* He just stood there staring at the man, trying to think of something to say. Now Ken registered Jack's pyjamas. 'Oh . . . sorry, I hope I didn't wake you. It's gone nine o'clock,' he added. 'So I thought . . .'

'Er . . . no, it's all right,' said Jack. 'We got in pretty late last night. But . . . I've . . . been up ages, actually. My dad's just . . .' He waved a hand towards the staircase. 'He'll be down in a minute.'

Ken smiled. 'Douglas phoned me last night and said you'd be here. I thought I'd just pop by and say hello.' He nodded towards the girl, who Jack now saw was holding a carrier bag. 'We brought you some eggs from the farm,' added Ken.

'Eggs?' gasped Jack, remembering the dream. 'Oh.'

'And some fresh milk.' Ken looked troubled. 'You *do* eat eggs, I hope?'

'Er . . . sure. As long as they're just . . . hen's eggs?'

Ken and the girl exchanged a puzzled look.

'What sort were you expecting?' asked Ken, amused.

At this point, Dad came clumping down the stairs, trying to look wide awake and failing badly. 'Oh . . . good morning,' he said. He came to the door and opened it a little wider. 'I'm . . . Michael. Pleased to meet you.' He reached out and the two men shook hands.

'Ken McFarlane. This is my daughter, Rhona.'

Jack noticed that the girl's face coloured up a little at the mention of her name. She kept her gaze fixed on the doorstep.

'Pleased to meet you both,' said Dad. 'You'll have to excuse Jack, he's half asleep this morning.'

That's a bit rich, thought Jack. He'd been awake before Dad, but he refrained from pointing this out. 'Douglas told me that you keep an eye on the place for him,' continued Dad. 'I'd love to offer you both a cup of tea but I'm afraid we don't have any milk . . .'

'Then it's a good job we brought some with us,' said Ken, jovially. 'That's very kind of you. We'll only stop a moment, though, we've work to attend to.'

'Er . . . oh, yes . . . please . . . any friend of Douglas . . .' Dad reluctantly opened the door wider and led the way along the hall. The two visitors followed him. Jack closed the door and trailed after them. In the kitchen, Dad waved the strangers towards the table and looked helplessly around. 'Now, I'm sure I saw teabags somewhere,' he muttered.

'Top cupboard,' said Ken, pointing. 'Just to your left, there, in the wooden caddy. This is very kind of you, isn't it, Rhona?'

The girl nodded, but her face remained expressionless. She took a large plastic container of milk from the carrier bag and set it down on the table.

'Straight from the cow,' said Ken. 'Full cream.' He winked. 'I won't tell anyone if you don't.'

Now Rhona pulled out a cardboard carton of eggs and set them beside the milk. 'Freshly laid this morning,' she said, speaking for the first time. Jack noticed that she had a lilting accent, much softer than her father's.

'That's really thoughtful of you,' said Dad. 'I'm afraid

we arrived too late to do any shopping last night. Luckily, the local chippie was open.' He took the milk and carried it over to the kettle, then started rooting around in cupboards to locate mugs and spoons.

'Douglas told me you were after a wee bit of peace and quiet,' said Ken. 'So we won't bother you too much.'

'Well,' said Dad. 'Yes, I . . . I've been working very hard on a big project. And Jack's had exams and so forth. We just . . . needed a bit of a break.'

'Er . . . yeah,' said Jack. 'That's right. A break.'

'Well, you certainly chose a good time. I can't remember when we last had such a long spell of hot weather. Hasn't rained in weeks . . .'

There was an uncomfortable silence.

'Jack, why don't you go and put some clothes on?" suggested Dad. 'You can't stay in your pyjamas all day, can you?'

'Oh . . . right.' Jack headed for the door, noticing as he did so that Rhona cast a sly sidelong look at him as he went by.

Up in his room, Jack put on his jeans and a T-shirt. He sat on the bed and pulled on socks and trainers. He could hear male voices talking animatedly in the kitchen below.

Before he went back down, he slipped into Dad's room and looked out of the window. Philbert remained in position, arms spread, gaze fixed intently on the house.

Again, Jack lifted a hand to try and get Philbert's attention and again there was no reaction. He felt abruptly rather foolish, reminding himself that he was trying to communicate with something that was almost certainly a hallucination. He shook his head, turned away and went back downstairs. Entering the kitchen, he saw that there was a cup of tea waiting for him in front of the one vacant seat. He settled himself down and automatically took a sip from his mug. The milk tasted rich and creamy, quite unlike the skimmed version he was used to at home. Ken was midway through some story, which Dad was listening to with rapt attention.

'So Douglas says to me, "Ken, something weird has happened." "Oh, what's that?" I ask him. "Well," he says, "we hung all the grouse on the washing line last night and when we got up this morning, they were gone. Vanished without a trace!" Foxes, of course. They'd taken every last one of 'em!'

Ken laughed uproariously as though it was the funniest story in the world, while Dad managed a polite chuckle.

'Imagine,' he said. 'You . . . get a lot of foxes around here, do you?'

'Some. But I'm told they're more of a nuisance in the city these days. From what I've heard, they're virtually taking over in Glasgow!' He paused to sip his tea. 'I'm afraid you've come at the wrong time of year if you fancied getting in a spot of shootin'. You can't pull a trigger until the glorious twelfth.'

Jack looked at Dad, bemused.

'The twelfth of August,' explained Dad. 'I believe that's when the grouse shooting season starts.' He smiled at Ken. 'Not really our kind of thing,' he continued, waving a hand at the locked gun cupboard. 'We prefer our poultry from the supermarket.'

'Aye, well, I can't say I blame you. I'll shoot the odd grouse for dinner, now and then, maybe even the occasional pheasant, but there are certain people in these parts who don't approve of that kind of thing.' He glanced slyly at his daughter. 'Can you imagine, a farmer's daughter who's a vegetarian? How did that happen, I wonder?'

The two men laughed conspiratorially and Rhona blushed again. Jack could see that she wasn't good with strangers and told himself it wasn't really a surprise, living out here in the middle of nowhere. She probably didn't get an awful lot of company.

'Animals have rights too,' said Rhona, quietly, her gaze fixed on her mug of tea. 'It's one thing to farm them for food and quite another to kill them for sport.'

Ken raised his eyebrows, then winked at Dad. 'You see what I have to contend with?' he said, with a grin. 'It's lucky for me I have a dairy herd, rather than a beef one, or I'd never hear the end of it!' He looked at Jack. 'Where do you stand on that one, Jack? Do you eat meat?'

'I had chicken and chips last night,' said Jack. 'But yeah, I get it. I don't think it's right to hunt animals for sport. Foxes, for instance. I think they're lovely. I'm glad they banned people from hunting them.'

He was rewarded with a smile from Rhona, before she looked away again.

'I think Douglas and his friends would disagree with you there,' said Ken. 'They lost a whole day's shoot to those fellows. They certainly didn't make the mistake of leaving their birds outside a second time.'

'At least the foxes would have eaten them all,' said Rhona. 'It's just wasteful to shoot so many birds in one day.'

Ken studied his daughter fondly for a moment, then

looked at Jack. 'You two must be around the same age,' he observed. 'You on your holidays too? Only I thought you English kids finished later than we do in Scotland?'

Jack didn't know what to say to that so he just shrugged.

'You should drop by the farm, some time, Jack. We'll show you around. I'm sure Rhona would be glad of the company.'

'*Dad!*' Rhona shot him a reproachful look and now she really was blushing. Ken ignored her protest.

'Seriously, though, any time. We're about half a mile up the road, first turning on the left. Twenty minutes' walk.' Ken lifted his mug and drained what was left of the contents. 'And now we really must get out of your hair. We've got a few things to do.' He stood up from the table and Dad did the same. The two men shook hands again and then they headed out of the kitchen towards the front door. Rhona stood up and looked at Jack.

'Sorry about my dad,' she murmured. 'He's always doing that.'

'No worries,' Jack assured her. 'And . . . maybe I will drop by sometime. That's if . . . it's OK with you?'

For the first time, she looked directly at him and he noticed now how blue her eyes were. 'That would be nice,' she said.

'Rhona?' Ken's voice was calling from the front door. She took a last gulp of her tea and then went out into the hall. Jack sat where he was, listening as Dad and Ken exchanged a few final words. Then there was the sound of the tractor starting up and Dad shouting goodbye. The door closed and Dad came back along the hall and into the kitchen. 'Well, they seem OK,' he observed. 'Bit too friendly, if you ask me. You notice the way he invited himself in for a cuppa? Couldn't really say no after him bringing the milk.'

Jack nodded. 'Yeah,' he said. 'They probably don't see many strangers. But they seem nice.'

'Sounded like you and Rhona were getting along pretty well.'

'Shut up,' said Jack, but he couldn't help smiling.

Dad picked up the cardboard carton and flipped it open, revealing rows of smooth brown eggs. 'These are beauties,' he said. 'How would you like them?'

Jack considered for a moment, thinking of the dream, remembering the multicoloured mouse-bird flapping frantically around the kitchen, but he pushed the memory aside. 'Scrambled,' he said and had another slurp of tea.

CHAPTER NINE
THE VILLAGE

After breakfast, Dad suggested they take a walk down the road to have a look around the local village.

'*Walk*?' muttered Jack. 'Why, is there something wrong with the car?'

'Don't be daft. We don't need it. The weather's lovely and it's less than half a mile, it'll do us good to stretch our legs for a change.'

'If you say so,' said Jack, unconvinced.

Just then, the phone in the front room started ringing. In the little room, the ringtone sounded incredibly loud. 'Maybe we should answer it?' suggested Jack. 'It could be Douglas.'

Dad shook his head. 'He told me he wouldn't use it.'

'But we don't have our mobiles! So how is he going to get in touch with us if he needs to?'

Dad frowned. 'He told me not to answer if it rang,' he said. 'He was very insistent about that. We have to wait until we've seen him.' The phone went on ringing for what seemed like ages and they both stood there looking at it anxiously before it finally stopped.

'Who was it?' murmured Jack. 'Who knows we're here? What if somebody's on to us?"

Dad shook his head. 'How could they possibly know where we are?' he reasoned. 'Douglas swore he wouldn't mention it to a soul.' Dad seemed to be thinking for a moment. 'It . . . it might just have been Ken,' he reasoned. 'Phoning to see if we needed anything else.'

They waited a while to see if the phone would ring again, but it didn't.

Ten minutes later, they let themselves out of the front door and walked along the track to the road. The sky was clear blue and the sun was already oppressive. Jack paused for a moment to unbutton his jacket. He watched as Dad crossed the road to stand by the wall. 'Whoa!' he said.

Jack followed and noticed that he was staring across the field, straight at Philbert. 'What's up?' he asked nervously.

'That has to be the ugliest scarecrow I've ever seen,' said Dad.

Jack winced, half expecting Philbert to react to the comment. 'Oh, he's . . . not so bad,' reasoned Jack.

'Not so bad? He's a *fright!* Like something out of a horror movie.'

'Hey, steady on,' said Jack. 'You'll . . . you'll hurt his feelings.'

Dad gave him an odd look. 'Oh right. And we wouldn't want to do that, would we? Hurt a scarecrow's feelings.'

Jack shook his head. 'No, it's . . . I just . . . I don't think he looks so bad, that's all. Quite . . . friendly, really.'

Dad chuckled. 'Oh, come on. If I was Ken I'd throw that thing on a bonfire and make a new one.'

'Don't say that!' snapped Jack. 'We . . . we don't want to get on the wrong side of him, do we?'

'Get on the wrong side of who?' he asked. 'Ken?'

'No, the . . .' Jack broke off, feeling ridiculous.

'The what? Jack, what are you talking about?'

'I was just going to say . . . the . . . the scarecrow?'

Dad snorted. 'Oh right. Because we don't want to hurt the feelings of a lump of old straw, do we? That would never do.'

'It was like . . . you know, a joke?'

'Right.' Dad gave Jack a suspicious look. 'Are you OK?' he asked.

'Of course, why wouldn't I be?'

'You tell me. Hey, you *have* taken your meds this morning, right?'

'Yes, of course,' snapped Jack, but it was a lie. He'd *thought* about taking them earlier and for some reason had decided against it. The problem was, he wasn't entirely sure why.

Dad turned to his right and started walking along the side of the road. Jack hurried after him and fell into step with him. Their boots crunched on the gravel-strewn tarmac.

'So, what's in this village?' asked Jack, eager to change the subject.

'Not very much,' said Dad. 'But we need to pick up a few bits and pieces to tide us over until Douglas gets here with some proper provisions. Well, we can't live on fish and chips, can we?' He glanced at Jack. 'Don't forget though, we're trying to keep a low profile. Don't go attracting attention or anything.'

'I'll try not to,' said Jack, wondering what Dad thought he might do once they reached the village. Start drooling at the mouth, maybe? Run around heaving bricks through people's windows? He took the opportunity to glance over his shoulder and saw with a twinge of dismay that Philbert was doing exactly the same thing, his head twisted round at an impossible angle. He was glowering after Jack and Dad with a pronounced scowl on his sacking features. Jack quickly looked away, not wanting Dad to follow his gaze and notice something odd. The next time he was able to sneak a look, Philbert had dwindled into the distance and was no more than a dark smudge in the midst of the corn.

'Douglas says the folks in the village are really friendly,' said Dad. 'Hopefully, they'll keep themselves to themselves.'

Jack nodded. 'Fingers crossed,' he said.

The narrow road wound along, high thick hedgerows on either side of it. They passed a turning to their left, which, Jack remembered, Ken had said led up to the farm, but it must have been well away from the main road because he could see nothing but fields on either side of the track. He and Dad kept on going. There was no pavement to walk on, but it hardly mattered because not a single vehicle went past them the whole way. After twenty minutes or so, they rounded a bend and saw what must be the village ahead of them, a row of white-painted buildings on each side of the road, looking almost dazzling in the sunlight. Dad pointed to the nearest of them. 'That's the chippie, where I went last night,' he said, as though giving Jack a guided tour. 'And that must be the local pub.'

It was a small, two-storey building with a thatched roof. A sign above the front door identified it as 'The Wolf in Winter'. The sign depicted a truly terrifying black wolf standing on a snow-shrouded hilltop, his muzzle wrinkled and pulled back to reveal jagged yellow teeth. Below him, in a narrow gully, several sheep cowered in terror waiting for the inevitable attack.

'Looks like a laugh riot,' observed Jack drily.

Dad chuckled. 'Evidently been here a long time,' he said, pointing to a date etched into the stone lintel. *1645.*

They wandered on and passed what appeared to be a newsagent's, though the yellowed books, papers and other assorted items ranged haphazardly in the shop window looked as though they had been lying there for centuries. There was a wire rack of newspapers by the doorway. Dad spent a bit of time thumbing through the *Guardian*, as though expecting to see his revelations in there. But despite looking carefully through every page, he eventually shook his head. 'I guess they aren't going to print anything until they know for sure it's genuine,' he murmured. 'And they can't do that until they've spoken to me.'

'Perhaps you should just ring them?' suggested Jack.

Dad shook his head. 'Douglas told me to do nothing until I've spoken to him,' he said. 'So I guess we'll have to wait.'

Jack shrugged. 'I didn't realise that Douglas was running this,' he said.

'He's not, but . . . well, I'd rather wait till I've spoken to him. He's my best friend and he's the only person I feel I can trust, right now.'

They walked on and came to the next shop in the row. 'Ah, now here's the general store,' said Dad.

'I can see that,' said Jack, pointing to a neatly stencilled sign that said exactly that.

'And that, I believe, is the petrol station,' added Dad, pointing up the road.

It wasn't much of a petrol station, a little wooden hut with just two rusty old pumps out in front of it, one for petrol, one for diesel. Jack saw that this was in fact the last building before the pavement petered out and the roadsides reverted back to wild hedgerow.

'Where's the rest of it?' asked Jack, genuinely bewildered. 'I mean, this can't be the whole village, can it?'

'I'm afraid it is,' said Dad. 'But let's face it, we didn't

come here for the crazy nightlife, did we?' He paused, as though expecting an answer, but when he didn't get one, he added, 'Let's check out the general store, shall we?'

'Oh, yeah, let's!' said Jack, trying in vain not to sound sarcastic. Dad led the way to the door and pushed it open, triggering an old-fashioned brass bell that clanged to announce their arrival. They stepped inside. It was essentially one big room with bare floorboards, the front part of it a maze of chest-high wooden shelving units that looked to Jack as though they'd been assembled sometime in the 1800s. At the top end of the room, a plump woman stood behind a dark wooden counter, smiling at them, as though she'd been expecting them to call. She was dressed in a spotless white coat, the kind of thing you might expect to see in a hospital, Jack thought.

Dad nodded to the woman and she nodded back, like the two of them were old friends. Dad collected a wire basket from a stack beside the door and led the way into the warren of shelves, which contained a selection of unexciting objects – tinned foods, packet foods, household goods, mops, brushes, bottles of shampoo, bleach, rubber plungers, tools, batteries . . . after a few moments, Jack zoned out and stopped actually seeing what was in front of him, but

Dad picked up the odd item and put it into the basket as he wandered around. Jack asked himself if this was all he had to look forward to for the foreseeable future. It was not an encouraging prospect.

'So, you're staying at Carlin Lodge,' said a voice beside him, making him start. The woman had come out from behind the counter and was needlessly rearranging some items on the shelf right beside him. Close up, she smelled of peppermints, Jack noticed, and she still had that serene smile on her rosy-cheeked face.

'How, er . . . how . . . how did you know?' stammered Jack. He was aware of Dad hurrying over to back him up.

'Oh, not much happens here that I don't hear about,' said the woman, brightly. 'Ken McFarlane dropped by this morning and he mentioned that there was somebody staying there again.' She turned and smiled at Dad as he approached. 'Mary MacCain,' she said, proffering a chubby hand. 'Everyone calls me Mary Mac. Pleased to meet you.'

'Er . . . likewise,' said Dad. 'I'm M— er, Martin.' Dad had obviously been about to give his real name but must have decided to change it at the last moment, which sounded really odd, Jack thought. 'Pleased to meet you. And er . . . this is my son . . . J-Joe.'

'Pleased to meet you, Joe. Up for a wee holiday, are you?'

'Something like that,' said Dad.

'So you must be friends of Douglas.'

'Er . . . yes, that's right,' agreed Dad. 'Old friends.'

'We haven't seen him in ages,' said Mary. 'But we so look forward to his visits. He always livens things up.'

'He's coming tomorrow!' blurted Jack and then, aware that Dad had given him a sharp look, added, 'I . . . er . . . I think.'

'Oh, now that *is* good news. Is he bringing more of his hunting pals with him? Angus over at The Wolf is always glad to see Douglas and his friends. He says business is never as good as when that lot are here!' And she laughed, a shrill little cackle that seemed to fill the entire shop.

Dad and Jack exchanged wary looks.

'It'll just be Douglas, this time,' said Dad. 'And he's not staying long. In fact, he'll be heading back to London on Sunday afternoon.'

'Oh, now that *is* a pity. Well, do tell him to pop his head in and say hello, while he's here. And be sure to let him know that my hubby, Angus, has got the special gun oil that he wanted.'

'I will,' said Dad. 'Absolutely.'

'And what about yourselves?'

'What about us?' asked Jack, bewildered.

'How long will *you* be staying?'

'We haven't really decided,' said Dad. 'City life was . . . er . . . getting on top of us. Thought we needed some peace and quiet.'

'You've certainly come to the right place for that,' Mary assured him. 'And you've lovely weather for it.' She gave Jack a sly look. 'Ken tells me that you've taken a bit of a shine to his daughter, Rhona. She's a lovely girl, don't you think?'

Jack didn't know how to begin to answer that question. He could feel his cheeks flushing. He looked hopelessly at Dad for help.

'Er, Mary,' said Dad, 'I was wondering . . .?'

'Yes, dear?'

'The er . . . the cottage. Why is it called Carlin Lodge?'

'Oh, bless you dear, that's because of the old Carlin Stone that stands in the field, nearby.'

'The . . . field with the scarecrow in it?' asked Jack.

'Yes, that's right, dear. Annie McFarlane made that scarecrow, before she . . .' Her voice trailed away for a moment. 'Oh yes, the Carlin Stone is well known in these parts. Been there since ancient times, it has.' She stepped closer and lowered her voice as though confiding a secret. 'There are people hereabouts who believe that it has special powers.'

'What kind of powers?' asked Jack, suddenly much more interested.

'Oh, well, it would take me a week to list them all. I wouldn't want to bore you with them.'

'I wouldn't be bored,' Jack assured her and Dad gave him a baffled look.

'Well, my mother used to tell me that it was a symbol of good fortune . . . that it could bring luck to people or even grant their wishes! But others will tell you that it's quite the opposite. Some believe that such stones are the home of the Cailleach.'

'The . . . what?'

'The Cailleach, dear . . . that's the goddess of the earth who's supposed to live in the very heart of the stone. She's the one who grants a good harvest, and brings the different seasons.' Mary laughed. 'In the olden days, people hereabouts even used to make sacrifices to her.'

'Why did they do that?'

'To make sure their crops would grow and that no harm should come to their loved ones.' She smiled. 'You have to take these old stories with a big pinch of salt, I'm afraid . . . though when I was a wee girl, I really did used to believe that it was a good-luck charm . . . not that the McFarlanes have had much of that over the past couple of years.' She shook her head sadly. 'Now, dear, was there anything else you needed?'

There was a short silence. 'Some . . . Cup-a-Soups?' ventured Dad.

'Of course, just round here. We have quite a selection.' Mary led the way back into the aisles and Dad threw Jack a look as if to say, 'You owe me one.'

Jack turned aside, remembering what Dad had said to him. 'Keep a low profile.' That was a good one! He was surprised that Mary hadn't known his age, blood group and what brand of underpants he preferred. He watched as Dad carried the wire basket over to the counter to pay for his shopping, Mary talking ten to the dozen the whole time.

'How will you be paying, dear? Only if it's a card, I have to make a wee charge. Oh, cash is it? Well, isn't that refreshing, there's not many who choose to pay like that these days, is there? Luckily, we're still allowed to take cash! There we are now, all done. And if it was a bigger shop you needed, here's our phone number, you can always ring us with an order and I'll get Angus to drop the things off at the lodge. We might not be Tesco Direct, but we try and do our bit! Now then, lovely to meet you both. Goodbye, Martin, goodbye, Joe!'

They let themselves out of the shop and both of them snatched an involuntary breath. Then they looked at each other and shared a chuckle.

'What was *she* like?' murmured Jack. 'I thought Douglas said people here kept themselves to themselves.'

'Oh, I expect she was just being friendly,' said Dad. 'I suppose it gets a bit lonely out here.'

'You think? What was the idea of giving false names?'

'I don't know, it just seemed to make sense.'

'But you already told Ken what we're really called. Supposing he goes in there and tells her?'

Dad frowned. 'I'm not very good at this secrecy stuff,' he muttered.

'You can say that again.' Jack leaned over and took one of the carrier bags of shopping. 'What do you suppose she meant about bad luck and the McFarlanes?'

Dad shrugged. 'Search me,' he said. 'And why were you so interested in that old stone?'

'I was just . . . being friendly,' said Jack.

'We don't want to get friendly with people like her,' Dad reminded him. 'She's too nosy by half.'

'OK, whatever you say. Where to now, do you reckon?'

Dad looked helplessly around. 'Back to the lodge?' he suggested. 'I think we've pretty much seen everything there is to see around here.'

Jack scowled. 'This is not a promising start.'

'Maybe we'll just have to accept that we need to take the car if we go out,' suggested Dad. 'I think I saw some maps back at the lodge. There's bound to be some interesting walks we could do.'

'Great,' said Jack. 'Walks.'

Dad sighed. 'Look, I'm sorry, Jack, I know this isn't much fun for you, but hopefully it won't be for too long.'

They walked back in near silence, sweating in the gathering heat of the day. Twenty minutes later, strolling alongside the field, Dad said, 'I see your mate is waiting for you.'

Jack glanced up. Philbert stood in the corn, staring resentfully at them as they went by. Whatever his mood might be, Jack didn't feel that it was particularly friendly right now, not after what Dad had said earlier. As the two of them went up the drive to the front door, Jack was already rehearsing the excuses he would give Philbert later on.

Jack was sure of one thing. Dad had a lot of enemies right now and he certainly didn't need another.

CHAPTER TEN
RHONA

Jack didn't have to wait too long before he could visit Philbert again. After an hour or so of lounging around, Dad announced that he was going to have a bath and trudged up the stairs out of sight.

Jack let himself out of the house and walked quickly along the drive to the road. As Jack entered the field and drew nearer, he noticed a slight movement. Philbert was glancing quickly to the left and right as if to ensure there was nobody around to observe things. When he brought his gaze back to focus on Jack it was evident from his expression that he wasn't in the best of moods. Indeed, he looked furious.

'What's the idea of coming here in broad daylight?' he hissed. 'I thought I told you that night time is best?'

'You *did* say that,' agreed Jack. 'But . . .'

'And I'm not even sure I want to talk to *you* again.

Not after this morning! Not after what your father said about me.'

'I thought you might be a bit hacked off,' said Jack, hoping to head off an argument. 'But look, he was only . . .'

'What a bloody cheek!' interrupted Philbert. 'Who the hell does he think he is, anyways?'

'Oh, he . . . he was only kidding around.'

'Was he really? Well, I'm afraid I didn't find it funny. He said he was going to tell Ken to put me on a bonfire!' Philbert's canvas face registered a look of horror.

'He . . . really didn't mean anything by it,' said Jack.

'Is that a fact?' Philbert shook his head. 'I don't know what a poor feller's supposed to do. Here I stand, minding my own business, trying to keep the field free of birds and then some blow-in like your father comes prancing along and says he'd like to see me set on fire.'

'Yes, but he doesn't know that you're . . .'

'What? Go on, say it. *Alive!* But he still wants to see me destroyed, doesn't he? I've a good mind to get him before he can talk to Ken.'

'What do you mean, "Get him"? You . . . you wouldn't hurt him, would you?'

Philbert sneered. 'I just might. And it would serve him right if I did.'

'Please don't do that,' pleaded Jack. 'I'm sorry. And I'll make sure he doesn't say anything to Ken. You just need to—'

'Hello?' The voice from behind Jack made him start. He wheeled round, trying desperately not to look guilty. Rhona was standing by the gate, looking across the field at him.

'Oh, er . . . hi!' said Jack. 'It's, er . . . it's Rhona, isn't it?' He started walking back towards her, pushing his way through the corn, grinning like an idiot.

'Can I help you at all?' she asked him. She was still wearing the much-too-big-for-her blue overalls, he noticed, and her red hair was tied back in a ponytail.

'Er . . . no, no, I'm fine. I was just . . .' He waved a hand in Philbert's direction. 'I was just . . . admiring the scarecrow.'

'Admiring him?' Rhona looked puzzled. 'It looked to me more like you were *talking* to him,' she said.

He laughed, a little too loudly. He leaned on the gate, trying to look relaxed.

'No, I was . . . er . . . studying him, actually. Yes, I'm . . . I'm kind of interested in scarecrows.'

'I see. They have a lot of them in London, do they?'

'No they don't. None at all. That's . . . kind of why I'm so interested. In the . . . the *tradition* of them and everything. The . . . workmanship. And Philbert there, he's one of the best I've ever . . .'

His voice trailed away when he saw her reaction. She took a step back from the gate and her expression registered shock. It was almost as though he'd slapped her. 'How did you know?' she whispered. 'How did you know his name?'

'I . . . er . . . I suppose you must have mentioned it,' he said. 'When you and your dad called round with the milk, yesterday? Yeah, that must be it. I think you said something about "Old Philbert" over in the field . . .'

But she was shaking her head. 'No, I didn't,' she said. 'I would never have done that.' She turned and started walking quickly away. 'I don't know who told you but it wasn't me.'

Dismayed by her reaction, Jack stood for a moment gazing after her – then hurried in pursuit. He had thought of another way out of it. He fell into step beside her. 'No, tell you what, I've just remembered. We went to the village earlier. Yeah. That woman . . . the one that runs the general store? Mary Mac? I think she told me.'

Rhona still looked puzzled. 'I didn't realise she knew,' she said.

'Oh yeah. She was telling me about the area and the Carlin Stone and everything. And she said, "Old Philbert in the field." That's where I heard it.'

Rhona scowled but after a few moments, seemed to accept the explanation. 'I suppose Dad might have mentioned it to her. He's always in there for a chat.' She seemed to think about it for a moment. 'That woman is the nosiest creature in Scotland,' she said. 'Once you've been here a week, she'll know everything there is to find out about you.' She looked at Jack with her startling blue gaze. 'And I do mean, *everything*.'

Jack frowned. So much for him and Dad keeping a low profile. 'Yeah, that's the impression I got,' he said. 'She was asking me all kinds of questions. Why were we here, how long were we staying . . .' He shook his head. 'So . . . I don't understand. What's the big secret? About the scarecrow's name, I mean?'

'It's not so much that it's a secret,' said Rhona. 'It's more that I haven't told many people about it.'

'Why not?'

'Well, if you must know, it was my mother's name for

114

him. She made him, you see. Maybe . . . eighteen months ago.'

'OK . . . and why Philbert?'

Rhona shrugged. 'She thought it suited him.'

Jack still didn't understand. 'OK, so your mother came up with the name. I still don't get it . . . what's the big deal?'

Rhona looked uncomfortable. 'Well, my mother's not with us any more.'

'Ah.' Now Jack thought that he was beginning to understand. 'I get it,' he said, thinking about his own recent experience. 'Oh, right. Welcome to the club.'

'I'm sorry?'

'Yeah, don't tell me, she met somebody else at work and then she ran out on your dad?'

'No,' said Rhona, looking shocked at the idea.

'Well, then, did she . . .?'

'She died,' said Rhona. 'My mother died. A year ago.'

There was a long silence after that, broken only by the clumping of their shoes on tarmac. Jack felt awful. Finally, he managed to break the silence. 'I'm . . . really sorry,' he said.

'Oh, don't worry. How were you to know?' She glanced

at him. 'So, is that what happened with your parents? They split up?'

Jack nodded. 'Yeah, pretty much. Oh, but it's OK . . . well, it is *now*, anyway. It was . . . hard to deal with at first. I think Dad's over it. I suppose we both are. But somebody dying, that . . . that must be worse. I don't suppose you ever get over something like that.'

'It wasn't the best time of our lives, that's for sure. I think Dad's come to terms with it. And I . . . well, I just miss her, you know. Like, all the time.' She looked miserable and for a moment, Jack was worried that she might be about to cry.

'So, er . . . where are we going?' he asked quickly, hoping to head off a potentially embarrassing situation.

She gave him a quizzical look. 'Well, I was headed back to the farm,' she said. 'I don't know where *you're* off to.' She stopped walking and they stood looking at each other for a moment, as though weighing each other up. 'But you're . . . welcome to come with me, if you like?' offered Rhona.

He didn't need asking twice. Anything was better than hanging around the lodge all day. 'Sure, why not? That would be really cool.' Jack glanced back towards the lodge. 'I'd maybe just better tell my dad first,' he added.

She smiled. 'Didn't realise you needed permission,' she said.

'Oh, I don't,' he assured her. 'But, er . . . he'll only worry if I don't tell him where I'm going. Wait for me, will you?'

'OK,' she said.

He turned and ran back to the lodge, aware of Philbert's eyes on him as he went past the field. He half expected to hear him mutter some sly comment, but the scarecrow must have been mindful of Rhona overhearing and kept his thoughts to himself. Jack went into the lodge and clattered up the stairs. He pushed open the bathroom door, releasing clouds of billowing steam. Dad was stretched out in the small bath, gazing up at the ceiling. He threw Jack an annoyed look. 'Where's a bloke supposed to go for some privacy around here?' he complained.

'Sorry, Dad. Is it OK if I walk up to the farm with Rhona?'

Dad sat up a little and gave him a knowing look. 'Rhona, is it?' he said and he grinned. 'My, but you're a quick worker.'

'Don't be daft. We just got chatting, that's all. Is it OK if I go?'

'I suppose. But Jack, remember, keep—'

'A low profile. Yeah, I know.'

'Don't tell them anything about why we're here, even if they ask. And don't stay there for ages!'

But Jack was already heading back down the stairs. When he reached the road he saw that Rhona had wandered back to the cornfield and was standing beside the gate, gazing at Philbert, who appeared to be looking straight back at her. And Jack wondered if Rhona actually knew about Philbert – about what he could do.

He crossed the road to stand beside her.

'Mum knew she was dying,' blurted Rhona, suddenly, not looking at him. 'It was cancer. She was really angry, you know, angry about all the things she was going to miss out on. And one day she asked Dad if she could have a wee bit of land of her own, somewhere she could just grow a crop. I don't know why that was so important to her, but it was what she wanted. Dad said she could have this field and for some reason, she planted maize. Worked really hard on it, too. And when the birds started coming to peck at the seeds, she made Philbert. Wouldn't let anyone else help her. She used to joke with Dad, said . . . that he was the other man in her life.'

Jack thought about that. Could it mean something? Had Rhona's mother known about Philbert?

'Of course, she was a witch, my mother . . .' said Rhona. She caught Jack's look of surprise and she smiled. 'Not *that* kind of a witch,' she added. 'I mean, she didn't go around wearing a big black hat and a cloak. She was Wiccan.'

'What's . . . Wiccan?'

'It's what they call a white witch. They're healers and they're supposed to be able to cast spells to help people get things they want – they help women have babies, and they make herbal cures for illnesses . . . stuff like that. She learned it all from my grandmother.'

'Does that mean . . .?' Jack pointed nervously at Rhona.

'Oh no, don't worry, I haven't followed in their footsteps. I can't do any of that stuff. Wouldn't want to! And Mum only knew a wee bit, you know. She . . . *dabbled*. It was Grandmother who had the big reputation.'

Jack nodded.

'So, after Mum was gone, Dad kept the field just the way it was. We planted a new crop this spring and kept Philbert there to guard it. When one of Douglas's friends took a pot shot at him, last August, Dad was furious. He told Douglas that the man who did it wasn't welcome here any more. I've never seen him so angry.' She shook her head. 'He wasn't like himself.' She turned and looked at

Jack and he saw that her blue eyes were shiny with tears. 'Was it hard for you when your mother left?' she asked him.

'I suppose so,' he admitted. 'But I kind of knew it was going to happen a long time before it did.'

'Yes, but so did I, with Mum. It didn't make it any easier.'

'It's not really the same thing,' said Jack. 'I . . . I expect your parents still loved each other? The problem was that my mum loved somebody else and my dad . . . well, I think he just didn't want things to change.'

Rhona nodded. She lifted an arm and dried her eyes on the back of her sleeve. 'Sorry,' she said. 'I must look a right mess. You still want to come up to the farm?'

'Sure,' he said and he smiled at her. 'Sure, I do.'

CHAPTER ELEVEN
THE FARM

Jack and Rhona walked in amicable silence. After all the serious talking they'd done earlier, Jack found it difficult now to think of something else to chat about. So they just strolled in the sunlight, thick green hedgerows on either side of them, the wide fields beyond. Apart from the occasional sound of birdsong, a deep silence prevailed. Finally, it was Rhona who ventured to speak.

'So, what do you make of it all?' she asked, waving a hand around her. 'The countryside, I mean? I expect it must be a bit of a shock to you?'

He nodded. 'It *is* kind of weird,' he admitted. 'I mean, it's so quiet here. I'm really not used to it.'

'You live in London, right?'

'Yes. Not in the city, mind. In a suburb. But it's always lively there, you know? Always something going on. There's a cinema just up the road. Cafes, coffee bars . . .

a park.' He looked at her. 'What do you do here for fun?'

She shrugged. 'I suppose we meet up with friends. We chat . . . walk. Stuff like that. It must sound pretty boring to you.'

'Not really,' he said. 'We do pretty much the same, only it's noisier. And, of course, we've got social media . . . can you even get a signal way out here?'

Rhona laughed. 'Of course we can!' she said. 'I like Instagram, myself.' She reached into the pocket of her overalls and pulled out an iPhone. 'We're not quite as primitive as you might think. Hey, maybe we should swap numbers?'

Jack tried not to look sheepish. 'I, er . . . I don't have a phone right now,' he said. 'I . . . dropped it, just before we left London. Haven't quite got around to picking up a new one yet.'

'You'll have to visit a town to do that,' she said. 'I suppose Pitlochry would be your best bet.' She smiled. 'I've always wanted to visit London,' she added. 'I've been to Glasgow and Edinburgh, of course, and they're lovely, but everyone says that London is an amazing place to shop.'

He chuckled at that. 'I suppose it must be,' he admitted. 'But I hate shopping.'

'I used to like going with my mum,' said Rhona. 'We

hardly ever bought anything, you know, we just liked trying clothes on and so forth. Having a good laugh. I can't really do that with my dad. He's tried but he hasn't got the first idea. He's more interested in power tools and stuff like that. And he never buys new clothes, I have to nag him to do it.' They walked on in silence again and then Rhona said, 'You *did* look like you were talking to Philbert.'

He threw a sly glance at her, trying to gauge what she was getting at.

'What if I told you I *was*?' he murmured. 'What would you say to that?'

'I'd get it,' she said. 'I've had the odd word with him myself.' Jack gave her a searching look and she seemed to speak defensively. 'Well, he's just somebody to sound off on, you know? You can talk about any old nonsense to a scarecrow, can't you?'

He shrugged. 'I guess,' he said.

'And, Mum used to talk to him all the time.'

'Did she?'

'Oh aye. She told me that she could speak to him about anything that was troubling her, things she could never tell Dad or me.'

'And did he . . .?'

'Did he what?'

'Oh, nothing.' He had wanted to ask if Philbert ever replied, but didn't want to sound like he was completely crazy. 'Do you . . . do you think there's anything special about Philbert?'

She gave him a scornful look. 'Of course. Haven't you been listening? He's very special to me and my dad.'

He nodded. 'Yeah, right.' He quickly abandoned the notion that Rhona might know anything about Philbert's abilities. It was clear that as far as she was concerned, he was nothing more than a collection of old clothes stuffed with cattle feed. And, Jack reminded himself, there was every reason to believe that she might be absolutely right about that.

Just then a battered green Land Rover appeared on the road ahead and sped towards them. 'That's Dad,' announced Rhona. 'Looks like he's in a hurry.'

The vehicle lurched to a halt alongside them and the driver's side window slid open. 'I was looking for you,' announced Ken, urgently. 'Thought you'd have been back ages ago. Out getting your head together again?' Rhona nodded uncomfortably. Ken nodded to Jack then turned his gaze back to his daughter. 'Well, one of our ladies is about to pop in the big shed. I thought you might be able to give me a hand.'

'Yeah, sure. Is it OK if Jack comes?'

Ken grinned. 'No worries. The more the merrier. Hop in, the pair of you.' Jack got in next to Rhona in the front of the Land Rover, wondering as he did so what he'd been invited to look at.

'Is it Sally?' asked Rhona and Ken nodded. He glanced at Jack.

'She insists on giving them all names,' he said. 'I tell her not to, but she pays me no heed. I don't suppose you've ever seen a calving before, have you?'

Jack shook his head. 'No,' he said. 'Maybe on the TV?'

'Well then, this will be a first for you,' said Ken. 'It's much better in real life.' He grinned ghoulishly. 'Messier.' He glanced at Rhona. 'So, you were a while,' he said. 'Did you manage to sort your head out?'

Rhona nodded. 'Kind of. And I bumped into Jack on the way back,' she said. 'He was talking to Philbert.'

'Was he now?' Ken looked amused. 'Well, that one's a good listener, I'd say. There's many a time I've had words with him, myself.'

'Really?' Jack looked at Ken, but the expression on the farmer's face said that he was only kidding.

They came to a narrow gateway on the left-hand side

of the road and Ken accelerated through it, the Land Rover bumping and skidding on the deeply rutted track. After a short distance, the farm came into view, a low, white, slate-roofed cottage and some outbuildings made from green corrugated iron. Ken brought the vehicle to a halt beside one of them, opened the door and jumped out. Jack followed his example, then looked down in dismay as his trainers sunk up to the ankles in a fresh cow pat. 'Oops,' said Rhona, trying not to laugh.

Ken was striding purposefully towards the nearest barn, so Jack extricated his feet as best he could and squelched after him.

'I can probably get you a spare pair of wellies from the house,' suggested Rhona, but Jack shook his head.

'It doesn't matter,' he assured her. He watched as Ken unlatched the big door of the barn and slid it aside. He gestured to Jack to follow him. The barn was huge. There was a central walkway with open stalls to either side, each one fronted by a metal gate. Only one stall had an occupant. A large, toffee-coloured cow stood in the corner of one stall, her head hanging down. She was lowing repeatedly, a deep, guttural sound as though she was in pain. Jack looked at her and then registered shock as he saw something sticking out of her back end – a pair of hooves.

'Oh my God,' he said. 'Is that . . . is that what I *think* it is?'

'It is indeed,' said Ken, gleefully. He took off his jacket and draped it over the nearest gate. 'This is Sally's first time, so she's going to need our help. Rhona, let's get her ready.' Ken opened the gate of the stall and he and Rhona walked in. Jack followed them at a respectable distance, overcome by the powerful smell, a mixture of cow dung and something that he couldn't quite identify. It seemed to fill his entire head and for an instant he almost gagged but he managed to get control of himself. As he watched, Ken and Rhona put their arms around Sally and led her over to a strange-looking metal contraption standing on the straw on the far side of the stall. It was a long steel frame with a handle sticking up from it.

'That's the calving jack,' said Rhona, and then, noticing Jack's puzzled expression, she added. 'I mean it's *called* a calving jack.' He noticed that the handle was attached to some long lengths of black chain. Ken and Rhona lifted the contraption and braced the blunt end of it against Sally's rear. Then Ken took the lengths of chain and began to attach them to the hooves that were sticking out from Sally's behind. Blood and mucous dribbled out around them and, once again, Jack felt his stomach lurch, but he was determined not to show himself up by being sick.

'The calf's coming out backwards,' announced Ken, as he worked, seemingly unperturbed by the slippery mess that now coated his hands up to his elbows. To add to his woes, a long fountain of greenish brown excrement poured out from just above the hooves and splashed onto Ken's wellingtons. He took no notice whatsoever and once the chains were properly attached, he simply wiped his hands on his already filthy jeans.

'Right,' he said, and he gave Rhona a thumbs-up. She moved to the other end of the contraption and pumped the handle a couple of times, making a sharp ratcheting sound. The lengths of chain tightened until all the slack was gone. 'OK, gently now,' said Ken. 'Jack, give her a hand, will you?'

Jack moved obediently to stand beside Rhona and she directed him to grip the handle with him.

'I'm not sure what to do,' he murmured.

'I'll show you,' she told him. 'It's easy.'

'OK,' said Ken. 'Give it a couple of pumps.'

Rhona cranked the handle and Jack did it with her, surprised, at first, by how much resistance there was. It was necessary to use all their combined strength to work the handle. For a moment, nothing happened but then, the legs suddenly slid out a few inches more, lubricated by a slick of blood and slime.

'Hold it a moment,' said Ken. As Jack watched, appalled, Ken got his bare hand into Sally's rear end and channelled some of the vile liquid out. 'Now, take up the slack. And . . . pull!' he said. They pumped the handle and the legs slipped out a little further. 'Excellent. Give it three good goes, this time.'

They heaved at the lever and now the calf began to emerge properly, a long skinny body, plastered in red and brown and yellow. The back legs were fully exposed but the body, skinny as it was, seemed to be stuck fast. Again, Ken told them to wait a moment and he repeated the exercise of channelling the worst of the mess away. He studied the half emerged calf thoughtfully. 'It's stuck pretty tight,' he announced to the shed in general, 'but a couple more goes should do it,' and he gave them another thumbs-up.

'OK,' said Rhona, looking at Jack and for the first time,

he saw the fierceness in her, the steely determination that hid behind that shy smile. 'Give it everything you've got.'

They cranked the lever as one, pulling hard and Jack was amazed at the resistance he felt, as though nothing was ever going to bring this new creature into the world; that it was going to die there, half exposed, unable to take its first breath.

'It . . . it's stuck,' he said. 'I can't . . .'

'Come on!' Rhona urged him and galvanised by her shout, he pulled with every ounce of strength he could find, his arm muscles straining, beads of sweat popping on his brow. And quite suddenly all the resistance was gone. The calf slid out completely and crashed to the straw in a great lolloping, leggy heap. If Jack had thought that would be the end of it, he was wrong. Ken immediately picked the calf up in his arms, oblivious to the mess it was making of his shirt. He carried it to the gate of the stalls and hung it over, hooking the haunches of its rear legs in position, so it could hang with its head down. Then he started to slap its sides and used his fingers to clear a slick of yellow mucous from its open mouth. For a moment there was no movement at all and Jack told himself that the process must have taken too long, that the calf had been stillborn.

But then it gave a kind of choking cough and a bawl and it spat out more fluid. Ken lifted it from the gate and laid it down on the straw again.

Rhona went over to Sally and led her to the calf. Sally nosed at her newly arrived offspring and began to lick away the yellow bag of mucous that still enclosed much of its body. Jack just stood there, open-mouthed in wonder, hardly believing what he had just seen.

Rhona stroked Sally's side fondly and then walked back to Jack. 'It's a girl,' she said and she smiled at her dad.

Ken studied the calf for a moment, his bloody hands on his hips. 'They'll be fine now,' he said. 'We'll let them get acquainted, shall we?' He turned away, grabbed his jacket and opened the gate. Jack and Rhona followed him. 'I'd better go and check on the rest of my girls,' announced Ken and strolled out of the barn, with the jaunty air of somebody who'd done nothing more demanding than a bit of shopping at the supermarket. Jack and Rhona remained where they were for the moment, leaning on the fence and watching Sally licking away at the newborn calf, which was already making clumsy attempts to get itself upright.

'What happens to her now?' asked Jack.

Rhona smiled. 'She's one of the lucky ones. She'll join

the dairy herd when she'd old enough. That's why I was so pleased it was a girl.'

'And if it had been a boy?'

Her smile vanished. 'The wee lads get sold for veal when they're just a few weeks old. There's a big market for it on the continent.' She scowled and he realised how difficult this must be for her. 'I can't change it,' she said, almost in her own defence. 'I've pleaded with dad, but in the end it's a business and selling off male calves is just part of it. But it's made me realise, I don't want to do this when I'm older. I'll work hard at school and get myself to a university. Dad wants it for me too. He says he'll sell up when he's ready to retire. He's nobody to pass the farm on to.'

'I suppose he might meet somebody else,' ventured Jack. 'He could have other kids.'

'That would never happen,' Rhona told him. 'Him and Mum were so close. I can't imagine him with anybody else.'

She turned and headed for the doors and Jack followed. As they stepped out into the open air, he was vaguely disappointed to see Dad's car parked on the road, a short distance away. Ken was standing by the car chatting happily. Dad noticed Jack and raised a hand to wave.

'Looks like I'm needed,' said Jack quietly, but he wished he could have spent longer with Rhona. He was just beginning to realise how much he liked her.

'Hey, mate, I noticed you forgot to bring your meds with you,' said Dad, waving a pack of tablets.

Jack gave him a despairing look. 'I took them before I came out,' he lied.

'Oh, sorry. But you can't be too careful, can you?'

'No, apparently not,' muttered Jack.

'Ken was telling me you just helped him deliver a calf.'

Jack snorted. 'I didn't do much,' he said. 'Rhona did most of the work.' He looked at her and smiled. 'Catch you later?' he said.

'Sure,' she said and she gave him that shy smile in return; but he was thinking of the way she'd looked earlier when she'd urged him to pull on that lever, the fire and determination in her. He hoped she hadn't heard Dad's comment about the meds, but didn't really see how she could have missed it. Something about her told him that she didn't miss very much at all. He opened the passenger door and sank into the seat beside Dad.

Dad gunned the engine, lifted a hand to wave and drove away. Jack looked back over his shoulder at Ken and Rhona, standing in front of the big barn, watching. 'So,' said Dad. 'Quite the farmer now, eh?'

But Jack didn't reply. He felt too annoyed with Dad. So he settled back in his seat, fixed his gaze on the road ahead and didn't say another word until they were back at the lodge.

CHAPTER TWELVE
ADVICE

Philbert seemed amused. He threw back his head and gave a hearty chuckle, then grinned at Jack, his eyes glinting malevolently in the moonlight.

'So you had to help deliver a wee calf. That must have been fun!'

'It was really messy,' admitted Jack. 'But kind of interesting. I've never seen anything like that before.' He glanced nervously in the direction of the lodge, half expecting to see Dad standing at the open doorway in his pyjamas, demanding to know what his son was doing in the middle of a cornfield in the early hours of the morning. Jack wasn't really sure why he was out here again, only that he hadn't been able to sleep and he'd really needed somebody to talk to. When he'd looked into Dad's room, he was sleeping soundly and when Jack walked to the window and looked across the moonlit

135

cornfield, there was Philbert, standing arms spread and gazing towards the lodge as if issuing a silent invitation. So Jack had put on his trainers and sneaked out, slipping a jacket over his pyjamas as he did so. Now the two of them stood in the silent darkness, Jack trying to come up with things to say that would mean something to a scarecrow.

'I didn't realise it would be so . . . yucky,' he admitted.

'I don't suppose you'd be used to that kind of thing,' mused Philbert. 'Coming from the big city and all. D'you have much contact with cows, there?'

'Only in McDonald's,' murmured Jack and when Philbert looked baffled, he added, 'It's a burger joint.'

'A what?'

'A place where you eat . . . er . . . cows,' said Jack, thinking that Philbert might not actually be familiar with the word 'burger'.

Philbert looked wistful. 'I've never tried cow,' he murmured. 'I bet they're nice. They *look* like they'd be tasty. Big, though.'

'You don't eat the whole animal!' Jack assured him. 'Just a bit of it. A slice, between two pieces of bread. To be honest, I prefer a chicken burger.'

Philbert gave Jack a meaningful look. 'I'm still waiting for that cooked chicken you promised me.'

'Yeah, well, it's not as easy as that. I need to be able to get out to the chippie. But Dad watches me like a hawk.'

Philbert lifted a stick index finger to scratch at his canvas chin. 'Why is that?' he wondered. 'Are you a wrong 'un or something?'

'No, of course not! If you must know, my dad's the one who's in trouble.'

'Oh yes, how's that then?'

Jack considered his reply before he spoke. He knew Dad had forbidden him to go blabbing to ordinary people but he thought surely he couldn't complain about his son confiding in a scarecrow. Could he?

'It's complicated,' he said. 'But basically, my dad found out some stuff about these people he worked with. They'd been doing something wrong . . . something illegal and he kind've told on them . . .'

'Ratted on them?' Philbert corrected him. 'I don't like the sound of that.'

'Well, yes, but, *they* were breaking the law.'

Philbert shrugged as though this meant nothing to him.

'So Dad passed their names on to the newspapers. Only

now, he reckons they might want to get even with him . . .'
He broke off in exasperation. 'I don't even know why I'm
telling you this! You're not real. I must be going mad.'

'Is that right? Then let me ask you something. Why do
you keep coming here, disturbing me in the dead of night,
if you don't even believe I'm real?'

Jack had to admit it was a very good question. 'I'm
just . . . trying to find out what's going on,' said Jack.
'Because if you're *not* real . . . if I'm imagining all this . . .
then I think I need to get some help.'

Philbert cackled at this. 'Well, you needn't think I'm
going to provide it. I've got my work cut out guarding this
field.'

'I don't mean that kind of help. I mean, like a doctor or
something.'

Philbert sneered. 'From what I've heard about doctors,
they're not worth listening to. I've heard Ken say that a
hundred times!' He shook his head. 'OK, so, you and your
rat of a father came here to hide.' He chuckled throatily.
'You're not on holiday at all. You're a pair of fugitives.'

'That's one word for us,' said Jack forlornly. 'But, hey,
listen, don't go telling anyone about this. Dad keeps saying
we've got to keep a low profile.'

Philbert blew out air from his pursed lips. 'Who would I tell?' he asked scornfully. 'You're the only person I talk to.'

'The only one you've *ever* talked to?'

'Yes, pretty much.' Philbert seemed to consider for a moment. 'I've spoken to mice occasionally.'

'Mice?'

'Yeah, just before I eat them. Well, it's only polite, isn't it, to say "excuse me", before you eat somebody?'

'I'll take your word for it.'

'And I spoke to an owl once, because he startled me one night by hooting in a tree right next to me. Woke me up, so he did. He wasn't much of a conversationalist though. I said to him, "I'm Philbert," and he just said, "Whoooo?"' He grinned his rotten grin. 'That was a wee joke, by the way. Feel free to crack a smile.'

But Jack was too preoccupied to even notice that Philbert had been joking. 'I've been thinking,' he said.

'Well, be careful. You don't want to strain anything.'

Jack ignored the remark. 'It's something that Rhona told me . . . about her mum. She said that it was her mum who made you in the first place.'

'Is that right? What, you mean like, put me together?'

'Yes. Around eighteen months ago.'

Philbert shook his head. 'Well, well. I didn't know that. I don't remember ever meeting the woman. I mean, I probably *did*, but she must have been well gone by the time I blinked awake. I've heard Ken and his daughter talking about her, saying how much they miss her and all but . . . I wouldn't know her if she walked right up to me and said hello.'

'OK. Well, she died about a year ago. She had this illness that was slowly killing her and she used to talk to you a lot, she used to tell you the things she couldn't say to other people.'

'Like what?'

'I don't know. About how she was feeling, I expect. And Rhona reckons that her mother was some kind of a . . . a witch.'

'A what?'

'A witch. You know, like someone who can do magic spells and stuff.'

'So?'

'So, do you think that something that Rhona's mum did, might have . . . helped to create you?'

'What kind of a question is that?' asked Philbert irritably.

'Honestly, you make my head hurt sometimes. I just . . .' He broke off as an upstairs light in the lodge clicked on. 'Hello, hello,' he said. 'Looks like your father's woken up.'

'I'd better get back,' said Jack, heading for the gate at speed, kicking his way through the dry straw. 'I'll have to tell him I couldn't sleep.'

'Fair enough. I've got better things to do anyways.'

'I'll see you again, soon.'

'Don't bother. Not unless you remember to bring me that chicken!'

'I'll see what I can do!'

Jack went through the gate, ran across the road and along the drive. He let himself in through the half open door, closing it quietly behind him. He hung his jacket on the hook beside the door and went straight to the kitchen, where he grabbed a glass off the drainer and started filling it with water. A moment later, the light snapped on. When Jack turned to look, Dad was standing in the open doorway of the kitchen, dressed in his rumpled pyjamas.

'Here you are,' he said. 'I got up to use the loo and you weren't in your room. I was worried.'

Jack lifted the glass of water. 'Just needed a drink,' he said. 'No big deal.'

Dad gave him a suspicious look. 'So why are you standing in the dark?' He looked down at Jack's feet. 'And why are you wearing trainers?'

'Trying to save electricity,' offered Jack. 'And . . . the . . . tiles are cold.' It sounded highly unlikely, but it was the only thing he could think to say. 'You OK?'

Dad grimaced. 'I had a dream,' he said. 'Well, more of a nightmare, really. I dreamed there were these people coming after us.'

'What kind of people?'

Dad shrugged. 'I'm not sure. They wore masks. Well, not masks exactly. They had these sacks over their heads.'

Jack took a big gulp of water and then turned back to the sink to top up his glass. 'I guess it's just anxiety,' he said.

'Maybe you're right.' Dad seemed to brighten a little. 'Douglas will be here tomorrow,' he said, as though that would solve all their problems. 'Hopefully he'll bring us some decent grub. I don't know about you but I'm looking forward to pigging out. Maybe he'll offer to cook. He usually does.' He turned away and headed back up the stairs. 'Try and get some sleep,' he advised Jack.

'I will.' Jack followed him across the kitchen and switched

off the light by the door. He was about to follow Dad up the stairs but something made him turn back to look at the window and the glass of water nearly dropped from his hand – because Philbert was standing at the window again, gazing in at him, his dark fathomless eyes burning into his.

'Sweet dreams,' murmured Dad, from the top of the stairs, as he headed for his room.

'You too,' croaked Jack. He waved a hand urgently at Philbert, telling him to go away and, after a few moments, the big shambling figure stepped back from the window and disappeared into the shadows. Jack turned away and headed up the stairs to his room, where he slammed the glass down on the bedside cabinet, got into bed and pulled the duvet up over his head.

Not surprisingly, he didn't get much sleep that night.

CHAPTER THIRTEEN

DOUGLAS

Douglas's midnight blue BMW came powering along the drive a little after midday. Dad and Jack had been listening out for his arrival for the past couple of hours and they hurried to the front door to greet him. The car lurched to a halt and Douglas leaped out, beaming at them from behind a pair of aviator-style shades. He was dressed in his regular weekend garb: a multicoloured Hawaiian shirt, baggy chinos and a pair of red Nikes.

'Hey, what's happening, guys?' he asked, breezily. 'I bring you warmest greetings from civilisation!'

Jack had always liked Douglas. He was Dad's oldest mate. The two of them had been at university together, though they were nothing like each other in temperament. Douglas was a short, heavyset fellow with a ruddy face and a head full of tight blond curls. He'd been captain of the rugby team at uni and still played a bit in his spare time for a variety of no-hope teams, but his fondness for several pints of real ale after every game had turned much of his former muscle into flab, particularly around the gut. He had a jolliness about him that was quite infectious, and Mum had often complained that he could bend Dad around his little finger. Mum had never really cared for Douglas. She thought that he led Dad on too easily, always inviting him out for 'drinks with the lads'. 'It's easy for him,' she used to say. 'He's got no commitments whatsoever.'

Douglas was what Dad called a 'player' but if that was the case, he clearly wasn't a very good one, since he had left a whole string of disastrous relationships in his wake. Jack had once overheard his parents talking about the real reason the last one had failed – something about Douglas's love of online gambling with which, it seemed, he had racked up considerable debts, without bothering to tell his partner. Mum had said she wasn't at all surprised, but Dad was always inclined to forgive Douglas for such failings, pointing out that 'Duggie' was a decent bloke who you could always go to if you were ever in trouble. Which is presumably why Dad had confided in him about the whistle-blowing thing.

Now Douglas was walking around to the boot of his car and was taking out the first of what looked like several cardboard boxes filled with provisions. 'Had to give the old credit card a bit of a bashing,' he roared, 'but I thought to myself, I can't leave my old mate and his son to survive on the slim pickings they'll find in Mary Mac's store now, can I?' He seemed to remember something. 'How come you guys didn't answer my texts?'

'Because Dad insisted on leaving our mobiles back in London,' said Jack, wearily. 'He reckoned they'd be traced.'

'Ah yes,' said Douglas. 'Well, that's actually a very sensible precaution under the circumstances.' He winked at Dad. 'Well done, Michael.'

Dad was already hurrying forward to help him. 'You didn't ring us yesterday, did you?' he asked. 'On the house phone?'

Douglas shook his head. 'Not me, old boy. You didn't answer it, I hope?'

'No, of course not. You told me not to.'

'Good. Well, I wouldn't worry too much. Could easily just have been a wrong number. Or Ken, seeing if you needed anything. He tends to do that.' He handed the first box to Dad.

'Thanks for this, by the way,' said Dad. 'I'll make sure you're sorted out, moneywise.'

'Don't even give it a second thought, old boy. Can't let my favourite whistle-blower starve, can I? Here, Jack, grab hold of this, will you?'

Jack stepped forward and took the second box. He couldn't help noticing that an awful lot of the 'provisions' that Douglas had picked up seemed to be of the alcoholic kind. Douglas must have caught Jack's doubtful look. 'Well, me and your old man have to allow ourselves the odd treat for good behaviour, don't we?' he protested. 'Or has he turned into a saint since he's been hiding out here?' He took the last box himself and slammed down the boot of the car with his elbow. 'Come on, let's get this stuff inside!' he suggested.

They went straight to the kitchen. Douglas slammed his cardboard box down on the kitchen table and started rummaging through the contents as if appraising them. 'Think I managed to cover all the major food groups,' he said. 'By the way, you lucky devils will be sampling my famous seafood spaghetti later on, something for which I'm sure you will both be eternally grateful. I'm not saying it's perfect, but it can only be a matter of time before *MasterChef* give me a call, know what I mean?' He beamed, then went to the kitchen cupboards and pulled out a couple of glasses. 'Now,' he said, 'it has come to my attention that

I've been here five minutes already and nobody has even offered me a drink! That won't do at all.'

Douglas lifted a large bottle of malt whisky from one of the boxes, uncapped it with a flourish and poured out two generous measures. He pulled a can of Coke from another box and handed it to Jack. 'Sorry, mate, can't let you have the good stuff, just yet. Come back in a couple of years,' he added, with a sly wink.

Jack smiled. He started unpacking his own box and carrying the packages over to the cupboards.

'So, how are things at work?' asked Dad warily.

Douglas gave him a meaningful look. 'I don't mind telling you, old son, things are hotting up at the office. People are looking nervous.'

'Anything in the papers?'

Douglas shook his head. 'Not yet! Well, they aren't going to publish what you've given them until they've had a chance to speak to you in person. They need to be sure of their sources, don't they?'

'So . . . when will I talk to them? I know we're in a mess here now, and I'm so sorry for dragging you both into this, but the more I think about it, the more I know it's the right thing to do. Those people are crooks!'

'You leave that with me. I'll set up a time and a place, when I'm sure it's safe for you to do so. It'll go to court, eventually, you mark my words – and I shouldn't be at all surprised if you're called upon to testify.'

'Really?' Dad looked worried at this news. 'Oh great.' He took a gulp of his whisky and grimaced as it went down.

'Don't sweat it, you'll be fine,' Douglas assured him.

'I suppose questions must already have been asked?'

'Of course they have! Giles Hunniford had me straight into his office, just as soon as you didn't show up for work. Asked me all sorts of things, didn't he? Did I know where you might be? "No idea," I told him. Did I know if there were any relatives you might be staying with? "Haven't a clue," I said. Had I heard anything from you directly? I looked him straight in the eye and told him I hadn't heard so much as a dickybird, but I made it clear that even if I *had*, there was no way he'd get anything out of me. He didn't like it much, but he had to suck it up.'

'You need to be careful,' Dad advised him. 'I don't want you jeopardising your own position with the bank.'

Douglas pulled a 'devil may care' expression. 'Tell you the truth, old son, I'm not sure I even want to stay in a job that's run by people like him and his cronies. Bob Hastings has been after me for ages to move over to his outfit. All right, so the pay's not quite as good, but at least I wouldn't feel like I needed to take a shower after every transaction.' Douglas had found a container of washing-up liquid in his box. He carried it over to the sink and set it down on the drainer. He stood for a moment, staring out of the window along the drive. 'I noticed that old scarecrow is still out in the field,' he observed. 'Stupid thing.'

Jack looked at him. 'Why do you say that?'

'Oh, it's just something that happened. Daft really.'

'What was it?' insisted Jack, though he already knew.

'I brought a bunch of pals up here to do some pheasant shooting last autumn . . .' He glanced at Dad. 'Before you say anything, I *did* ask you along, but naturally Catherine wouldn't let you come out to play . . .'

'That's not what happened,' protested Dad. 'It clashed with something else.'

'Yeah, Catherine doing her hair or, Catherine painting her fingernails, something really *important* like that.' Douglas rolled his eyes and then glanced apologetically at Jack. It was no secret that he and Jack's mum had never really got along. 'Anyway, old Johnny Reilly was there and you know what Johnny's like when he's had a couple of drinks.' Douglas chuckled at the memory. 'Only went and took a pot shot at the scarecrow, blew a hole right through it!' Douglas tilted back his head and guffawed loudly. 'Just a bit of a laugh, you know, but the next thing, old Ken comes storming up to us demanding to know what the hell we're playing at and generally carrying on as though we've committed some kind of crime. I said to him, "Ken, old son, calm down, it's not like we're damaging anything valuable is it?" And he looks at me and says—'

'His wife made it,' said Jack, without thinking.

Douglas turned to look at him. 'Beg pardon?' he muttered.

'Ken's wife . . .' Jack remembered that Mary Mac had mentioned the woman's name. 'Annie, I think she was called, she was ill, you see, dying of cancer. And she built Philbert . . . that's what she called the scarecrow . . . and Ken has kind of kept him there ever since to . . . remind him of her.'

Douglas's mouth was hanging open. He made an effort and closed it. 'Oh goodness, I . . . I had no idea,' he said. 'But it's not as if it's worth—'

'It means a lot to Ken and Rhona,' said Jack, forcefully. 'They think of him almost like one of the family.'

Douglas turned his gaze to Dad as though seeking help.

'I think Jack's a bit sweet on Ken's daughter,' announced Dad, as if that explained everything.

'I'm not "sweet on her",' protested Jack. 'But she's a friend, so . . .'

'A friend, eh?' Douglas seemed to shrug off his momentary discomfort like a sweater that didn't fit him properly. He gave Jack an exaggerated wink and Jack felt like punching him. 'You're a fast mover! Well, I get the picture.' He tapped the side of his nose. 'Say no more! Already developing an eye for the young ladies, eh?' He gave Dad a withering look. 'He clearly doesn't take after you!'

Dad laughed at that, though Jack didn't feel it was a particularly nice thing to say. Douglas turned away from the window and came back to the table. 'Anyway, where was I?'

'The office?' prompted Dad.

'Oh yeah, so poor old Giles is just about doing his nut trying to find out something about you. But he's stymied, isn't he? He hasn't a clue about this place, I've always kept it to myself.'

'But you said you invited friends,' Jack reminded him.

'Yes, but only people I know I can trust. And, more

importantly, *not* people from the bank. I always say to the lads who come here, "Let's keep this place our little secret." And not just because I don't want to pay any tax on it!' He winked at Jack. 'So my advice is, you two continue to keep your heads down, until such time as we know what's happening with the investigation. Then I'll organise getting you to the right people. You just leave everything to your old Uncle Duggie.'

Dad looked worried. 'How long do you think it'll take?' he asked.

'Hard to say, old son, hard to say. Obviously I'll keep you posted. Not sure how we'll do that without mobiles. Maybe you could just pick up a cheap Pay As You Go so I can text you? Like they do in the spy movies, eh? But for the moment, we need to make sure that nobody finds out where you are.' Douglas gave Dad a searching look. 'So, er . . . listen . . . have you told anybody else? About here.'

'No, not really . . .'

'Not really?' Douglas looked impatient. 'Please tell me you haven't spoken to Catherine. You know what she's like, it'd be all over Facebook before you could turn around and fart.'

'No, I haven't said anything to anyone. Not yet. But . . . I've been thinking, Duggie, maybe I *should* get in touch with her. I mean, what about Jack? Catherine is going to find out about this sooner or later. I left a message on the school answerphone just before we left, saying that Jack was ill but it won't be long before people start asking questions and—'

Douglas waved him to silence. 'Trust me on this. We need to keep your presence here under wraps. I suppose you've already spoken to the locals?'

'Well, Ken, of course . . . and his daughter. And we did meet that Mary Mac at her shop.'

Douglas didn't seem worried by this. 'She's nosy but harmless. Social media is the thing to avoid. The adults around here wouldn't know it if it jumped up and bit them.' He glanced at Jack. 'If Rhona uses it, tell her on no account is she to stick you on Facebook or Twitter, OK, even if the two of you *are* going out together.'

'We're not going out!' protested Jack.

'Yeah, whatever. Let's have no selfies down on the farm, all right? Let's have no "hashtag meetmynewboyf!" You haven't done anything like that already, I hope?

'No nothing.' Jack thought for a moment. 'I did . . . help her deliver a calf, yesterday.'

154

'Deliver it *where*?' asked Douglas, mystified.

'No, I mean . . . you know . . . I helped it to be born.'

'Eww.' Douglas made a face. 'Well,' he concluded, 'I suppose people have to make their own entertainment out here, don't they?'

'It was pretty cool, actually.'

'Yeah, whatever. Like I say, make sure nobody else knows where you are. The two of you just need to hunker down, keep quiet and wait this out. It'll be worth it in the long run.'

'So when do you reckon we'll be able to go home?' asked Jack.

Douglas shrugged. 'Who can tell? Something like this takes time. The important thing is that we keep you both safe. It's a brave thing your dad did. Some would say a foolish thing, but hey, you can't have everything. And, you know, if we handle this right, he could come out of this a hero.' He grinned, picked up the bottle of Scotch, and refreshed the drinks. He lifted his glass. 'Here's to doing the right thing,' he said.

'Cheers,' said Dad, and they both drank.

CHAPTER FOURTEEN
DINNER IS SERVED

The afternoon wore gradually into evening. At Jack's request, Douglas unlocked the gun cabinet in the kitchen and showed Jack the two shotguns he kept in there: big, brutal-looking weapons that smelled strongly of oil. Douglas lifted one out and handed it to Jack, let him feel the unfamiliar weight of it in his hands. It seemed to weigh a ton. Dad stood in the doorway, watching, and sipping at his glass of whisky.

'Can't let you fire it I'm afraid,' Douglas told Jack. 'Not even in the garden. There are strict rules about it. You're not allowed to fire a shot until the . . .'

' . . . glorious twelfth,' murmured Jack, remembering what Ken had said, when he was talking to Dad. 'That's OK, I don't really want to fire it. I just wanted to see what it looked like.' He frowned. 'Why do you need such a big gun to kill such a small bird?'

'They're not *that* small,' Douglas assured him. 'You can feed two people royally off one pheasant. But . . .' He gestured at the ends of the twin barrels. 'The shot spreads as it fires, you see. It means there's less chance of missing.'

'That's not very sporting,' observed Jack.

'Who says it has to be sporting?' muttered Douglas. 'This is all about eating delicious food.' Then he seemed to remember something. 'Ah, of course,' he said. 'Ken's girl's a bit of a hippie, isn't she? Opposed to hunting and all that malarkey. Lord knows how Ken puts up with it on a farm.'

Jack scowled. 'I think she's entitled to her opinion,' he argued.

Douglas glanced knowingly at Dad. 'Oh, watch out, Michael. Looks like this one's got it bad.' He took the shotgun from Jack and put it back in the cupboard, then made a big thing of padlocking it shut. 'You must always keep this locked,' he said. 'Guns are dangerous and we must respect them.'

'Maybe I'll come along, next time you organise a shooting party,' said Dad, enthusiastically. The alcohol was clearly already having an effect on him, Jack thought. He'd normally run a mile rather than volunteer for something like that.

Douglas grinned. 'You just say the word, old boy, and it's done. We'll make a sharpshooter of you yet. Now then!' He clapped his hands together. 'Time to start cooking, I think!'

'Already?' Jack glanced at his watch. 'It's only three o'clock.'

'Ah, but you have no idea the amount of preparation that goes into my seafood spaghetti,' insisted Douglas. 'It's like a military operation.'

He wasn't exaggerating. Jack and Dad were banished to the sitting room while Douglas set about creating what he kept referring to as his 'culinary masterpiece'. The process seemed to involve much crashing about in the kitchen, the production of great clouds of steam and the use of just about every pan on the premises, but when it was finally ready to be served up, Jack had to admit it *did* look pretty amazing, even though there seemed to be enough to feed an army. By the time the three of them sat down at the small dining table in the front room, Douglas and Dad had drunk their way through the best part of a bottle of Scotch – though it seemed to Jack that Dad had drunk a good deal more than Douglas, who was only sipping at each glass.

'Don't stand on ceremony,' suggested Douglas. 'Dig in.'

Jack was happy to take him at his word. Apart from the fish and chicken and chips they'd had the first night, meals at the lodge had consisted mostly of sandwiches and packet soups, none of which had proved satisfying to Jack's healthy young appetite.

He ate ravenously, cramming the spaghetti into his mouth in great dollops and gulping it down. As he ate, Douglas gave him a running commentary on what was in the dish, explaining how important it was to get exactly the right mixture of garlic and pesto, and how the pasta had to be boiled for exactly eleven minutes and forty seconds, to produce that perfect texture. Dad ate more sparingly than his companions and Jack could see that he was clearly worried about what he and Douglas had discussed earlier.

When they had all eaten as much as they could, Douglas surveyed the big mound of pasta still left in the bowl and shook his head. 'We hardly did justice to it,' he said. 'Are you guys sure you can't eat any more?'

'I'm stuffed,' said Jack, 'but it was really good.'

'Well, don't worry, it'll heat up,' said Douglas. 'A few minutes in the microwave and you've got yourself another easy dinner.'

'That's great,' said Dad. 'Thanks, Douglas, I don't know what we'd have done without you. I really owe you one.'

'Nonsense. My pleasure.' Douglas waved a hand in dismissal and then stood up from the table. 'And with that, I'll take myself outside for my usual post-prandial cigarette.'

'Sorry to see you're back on them,' said Dad. 'I thought you'd given up.'

'Tried a hundred times, can't quite manage to do it.'

'And you don't have to go outside,' Dad told him. 'Smoke in here. Heck, I might even join you for one.'

'No way! It's an absolutely filthy habit and I'm not going to be the one to put temptation in your path.' Douglas stood up from the table. 'Back in a mo,' he said.

Jack and Dad sat in silence for a while, Dad toying with a few leftover strands of spaghetti still wrapped round the end of his fork. He seemed to be deep in thought.

'I'm sorry about all this,' he said at last and Jack noticed that his voice was a little slurred. 'I'm sorry I got you involved. I should have thought carefully about it before I spilled the beans. I didn't stop to think about how this would impact on *you*.'

'Oh, that's OK,' Jack told him.

'No, it's not, not really.' Jack was shocked to see that Dad was close to tears over this. 'I was just so angry at Catherine and I . . . I was stupidly reckless. I acted without a single thought for anyone but myself. Now I've dragged you all the way out here to a tiny cottage at the back end of nowhere. You must be bored out of your mind.'

'Actually, it's been a lot more interesting here than I expected.'

Dad seemed to brighten a little at this news. He gave Jack a knowing look. 'You mean Rhona?' he asked.

Jack felt a jolt of irritation. 'No, that's not it. Why do adults have to make everything about *that*? There are other things, you know!'

'Like for instance?'

'Like . . . the farm and stuff. Watching that calf get born, that was pretty cool. I mean, you wouldn't see that in London, would you?'

'I suppose not.' Dad seemed amused by Jack's defensiveness. He gave him a sly look. 'Rhona does seem nice though, doesn't she?'

Jack shrugged. 'Yeah,' he admitted. 'Yeah, she's OK.'

Dad looked thoughtful. 'What were you saying to

Douglas before about that scarecrow? About it being one of the family? That's a bit weird, isn't it?'

'You have no idea,' said Jack, shaking his head. 'This place is weird in all sorts of ways.'

Now Dad gave him an odd look. 'You er . . . you *have* been keeping up with those meds, haven't you?' he asked.

'Er . . . sure,' said Jack, but it wasn't true. He hadn't even thought about it since the first day he'd arrived here.

'We'll need to sort something out soon,' said Dad, thoughtfully.

'Hmm?'

'About the meds. I mean, I know this place is remote but there must be a local doctor who can do a repeat prescription for you.'

'Oh, don't sweat it,' Jack told him. 'Really, I've got plenty.' He was about to say something else, but he broke off as he noticed something odd. 'That's funny,' he said.

'What's funny?'

Jack pointed to the mantelpiece above the fireplace. Douglas's cigarettes were there, exactly where he'd put them when he'd first arrived. 'I thought he said he was going outside for a smoke.'

Dad chuckled. 'The idiot! He must be drunk.' He waved

a hand towards the fireplace. 'Here, take them out to him,' he suggested. 'I'll get stuck into the washing up.'

Jack collected the cigarettes and Zippo lighter and went outside. He'd expected to find Douglas standing in the light of the porch, but he was nowhere to be seen. Puzzled, Jack looked along the drive towards the road and he finally spotted Douglas, standing by the wall bordering Philbert's field. He was walking up and down, talking urgently into a mobile phone. Jack started walking towards him and as he drew closer, Douglas turned in his direction and saw him coming. Jack held up the packet of cigarettes and Douglas's face went through a series of expressions, as though he was trying each of them for suitability. First a look of shocked surprise, then an embarrassed grin as he registered the cigarettes and finally, a rolling of the eyes as he acknowledged what a dope he was. He said something into the phone, then slipped the handset into his pocket.

As Jack crossed the road to him, he started talking. 'That was Jenny, my assistant from work,' he said. 'She was asking me about some bloody files she'd mislaid. As if I'd have any idea where they were! I've told her repeatedly not to bother me on a weekend, but does she take any notice? No she does not!' He took the cigarettes and lighter from

Jack and fumbled a smoke out of the packet. 'Honestly, I'd forget my head if it wasn't screwed on. I stepped outside and realised straight away I'd forgotten the fags . . . and I was just about to come back in when the bloody phone rang, and it was Jenny. So I thought I'd better come away from the door, just in case you heard me shouting at her. I don't want the word going around that I'm some kind of bully, do I?'

Douglas laughed, lifted the cigarette to his lips and lit it, shielding the flame with his hands. He blew out a cloud of smoke. 'Don't you go getting into these things, young Jack,' he continued. 'Been the blight of my life, they have. Tried hundreds of times to kick 'em, just can't quite manage to do it.' He seemed to realise that he was blathering and paused. 'You . . . OK?' he asked.

'Sure,' said Jack. He didn't quite know now if he should go back to the lodge or if he was expected to stay and talk. He decided on the latter. 'So . . . how much trouble is Dad really in?' he asked.

'Oh, well . . . obviously, there are a lot of powerful people who are pretty angry with him right now, but . . . like I said, provided he keeps his head down, it should blow over soon enough.'

'They wouldn't . . . harm him, would they? These powerful people? It's not like he's some kind of . . . target?'

Douglas looked at Jack for a moment and then scoffed. 'Oh no, it wouldn't come to that. Goodness me! It's not like we live in . . .' He waved a hand as though trying to think of somewhere suitably lawless, but he failed to come up with anything. He looked around as if seeking inspiration and his gaze fell on Philbert, standing arms outstretched in the centre of the field. 'Sorry about what I said before,' he murmured. 'I knew about Ken's wife dying, of course, but he's honestly never said anything to me about the scarecrow. No wonder he was annoyed.' He took another drag on his cigarette. 'You have to admit though, it is an ugly-looking thing.'

Jack frowned. 'Everyone says that,' he admitted. 'But he's actually not so bad when you get used to him.' He looked at Douglas intently. 'I wanted to thank you,' he added.

Douglas seemed surprised. 'Thank me for what?' he asked.

'Just for being there when Dad needed help. I don't know what he'd have done without you.'

'Oh, that's . . . it's nothing. Really. I'm glad to have been of service.' Douglas was staring off across the field at the scarecrow. 'Me and your dad, we go back a long way. I used to defend him whenever he got into fights at uni.'

Jack was intrigued. 'Dad used to get into fights?' he murmured.

'Oh yeah. Not often, mind you. And not his fault, either. He was kind of skinny and there were some people there who tried to push him around. So I'd step in and . . . fight his corner, you know? He . . . he knows I've always got his back.'

'OK. Well, I just thought I'd say thanks anyway.' Jack turned and started back towards the lodge. 'I'll go and give him a hand with the washing up,' he said.

'Yeah, no worries. I'll just finish this and I'll be right there.' Douglas waved his cigarette. 'I . . . think there's sticky toffee pudding and custard for afters.'

'I'm too full,' said Jack.

'Well, maybe later, eh? And I just remembered, there are board games in a cupboard somewhere. Maybe we could play *Trivial Pursuit* or something like that?'

'Sure.' Jack strolled back across the road. When he paused at the top of the drive to glance back, Douglas had turned away and was staring across the field at Philbert. The scarecrow was looking straight back at him. For a moment, it occurred to Jack that the two of them might be in cahoots, that as soon as Jack had gone inside, they'd start chatting to each other. But he quickly dismissed the idea. After all, Philbert had assured him, Jack was the only one who knew the secret.

He strolled up the drive and let himself into the lodge, leaving the door ajar so that Douglas could easily follow him inside.

CHAPTER FIFTEEN

A WARNING

Jack was dreaming. He knew it was a dream and yet, that didn't make it feel any less terrifying. He was running through a forest at night, the grey trunks of trees rearing up on either side of him in the gloom, a dark rustling canopy of leaves high overhead and he wasn't running for pleasure, no, he was running for his life because something . . . something he couldn't see, was following close on his heels. He could sense that it was big and powerful and he could hear the great animal grunts it was making as it came in pursuit, crashing headlong through the shrubs and bushes behind him. He knew only too well that if the thing caught up with him, it would tear him to pieces; that he would die here alone in this deserted place, with nobody to help him . . .

He woke suddenly, convinced that a real sound had just cut into the dream, a sharp staccato click. As he lay in his bed, staring blankly up at the ceiling, it came again. Something small and hard had just smacked against the glass of his bedroom window. He glanced at the clock on his bedside cabinet and an illuminated display told him that it was just after midnight. Puzzled, he shrugged off sleep, struggled out of bed and went to the window. He pulled back the curtain and saw to his surprise that Philbert was standing in the back garden below, frozen in the act of throwing another pebble. He stared up and beckoned urgently to Jack, clearly telling him to come down.

Jack went to open the window in order to talk, but thought better of it. Dad was a heavy sleeper but Douglas, who was kipping on the sofa in the front room, might hear something and come to investigate. That would never do. So Jack put on his trainers and crept out onto the landing. He glanced into Dad's room as he went by and assured himself that his father, his senses dulled by all that whisky, was indeed out cold and snoring.

Jack went down the creaky wooden stairs, placing his feet with great care. He quietly opened the door of the front room and peered inside. He was surprised to see that there was nobody lying on the sofa, which seemed odd.

Where was Douglas? Had he gone outside for another cigarette? If so, there was a real danger of him spotting Philbert standing in the garden.

Jack slipped on his jacket, switched on the porch light and cautiously opened the front door. He looked outside. It was kind of misty, but he saw instantly that something wasn't right. Dad's car was in its usual spot but there was no sign of Douglas's BMW, even though he wasn't supposed to be leaving until the afternoon. Just then, Philbert came striding round the side of the house. He opened his mouth to say something but Jack lifted a finger to his lips and pointed along the drive towards the road. The two of them walked in silence until Jack judged that they were far enough away from the lodge for their conversation to go unheard.

'What's going on?' he demanded. 'Where's Douglas's car?'

'That's a very good question,' said Philbert. 'He drove off a few minutes ago. Took his bag with him and everything. Crept out like a thief in the night, he did. I saw it all from the field.'

Jack frowned. 'But why would he do that?' he murmured. 'He told us he was staying until the afternoon.'

'I wouldn't take his word for anything,' growled Philbert.

'He's the one who lets his friends use innocent scarecrows for target practice.'

'Yes, but if there was a change of plan, surely he would have woken us up and told us?' Jack thought for a moment. 'That phone call he had earlier on,' he murmured. 'Maybe it was something to do with that. He said his assistant rang him. Somebody called Jenny? Maybe she rang again, and said he was needed back in London.'

Philbert shook his head. 'I know that's what he told you.' He leaned sideways and spat. 'He lied.'

Jack stared at him in surprise. 'What do you mean?'

'Nobody rang *him*. He's the one that made the call.'

'Are you . . . sure?'

'Of course I'm sure! I saw everything, didn't I? Heard it too. I wanted to warn you earlier but I couldn't take the risk of him seeing me. I kept peeping in the window of the lodge and every time I did, he was just sitting in the front room, wide awake, looking at his phone.'

Jack glared at Philbert. 'What do you mean, you wanted to warn me? About what?'

'I don't know for sure, but something here doesn't smell right. Do you trust that man? It wasn't a Jenny he was speaking to. It was somebody called Giles.'

'Giles?' Jack gasped. 'Not . . . Giles Hunniford?'

Philbert shrugged his big shoulders. 'I didn't hear any other name. Just the first one. Giles.'

'You . . . you must be mistaken.'

Philbert shook his head. 'There's nothing wrong with my hearing. The red-faced feller made the call and he said something like, "Hi Giles, it's me." And then he said something like, "Aye, everything's ready. There's just the two of them." And then he listened for a bit and said, "No, they haven't told anyone they're staying here."'

Jack drew in a breath. 'Did he say anything else?'

'Plenty. He said, "Just promise me there won't be any loose ends."'

'Loose ends?' Shock waves were pulsing through Jack's head and he was desperately trying to decide what he should do next. 'What could that mean?'

Philbert shrugged his massive shoulders. 'Then the red-faced feller listened for a wee bit longer and he said something about money. He asked this Giles to promise him that, "the money would go straight into his account," whatever that means. And he said something about how Michael was his oldest friend in the world and he wouldn't ever have considered doing this if he wasn't absolutely desperate, but so long as Giles could assure him that there would be no loose ends, then the two of them had a deal . . . and then he started to give the address of the lodge, but that's when you came out with his cigarettes. After you'd finished talking and went back inside, he dialled the number again and finished giving the address. And then he said, "Over to you."'

Jack felt like he was waking up all over again. Alarm bells were going off in his skull and he felt mesmerised by them.

'I . . . I don't know what to do,' he said. 'I think this means that people are definitely coming after us . . . probably soon, if Douglas has cleared out. Maybe he didn't want to be here when it all kicks off.'

'When *what* kicks off?' asked Philbert.

'I don't know. But I think people will be coming here. People who want to get my dad. Silence him.' He reached out and grabbed Philbert's arm. He was momentarily startled by how powerful it felt. 'What should we do?' he implored.

'If I were you I'd get out of there,' said Philbert. 'You're sitting ducks as long as you stay in that place. I'd make a run for it.'

'But where would we go?'

Philbert thought for a moment. Then he turned and looked towards the field. 'The forest,' he said. 'On the far side of the field.' He pointed a stick finger. 'It's deep enough to hide from just about anything.'

The dream came back to Jack then, the image of him running through the woods at night pursued by something unspeakable. 'I . . . I wouldn't know which way to go,' he said desperately.

'I can guide you,' said Philbert. 'I know that place like the back of my hand.' He clamped his wooden fingers onto Jack's shoulder and shook him, in an attempt to make him focus. 'Go and wake your father up. Tell him you have to leave, right now. Take only what the two of you can carry. But whatever you do, don't hang about.'

'What will I tell him?'

'The truth,' Philbert assured him. 'As soon as you're ready, cross the field and head into the woods. I'll come and find you when I know what's happening. Hurry, now. I'll keep a watch on the road.'

Jack nodded. He turned and ran back to the lodge, as fast as he could go. He let himself in and pounded up the stairs to Dad's room, no longer worried about making any noise. He ran into Dad's bedroom, yelling like a maniac. 'Wake up!' he bellowed. 'WAKE UP! We've got to get out of here, NOW!'

Dad woke suddenly, his eyes wide, his mouth open. He looked scared and he had every reason to.

'Jack, what the—?'

Jack went to the bed and leaned over him, looking straight into his eyes. 'I haven't got time to explain, but we have to get out of here. Do you understand? You need to get up and be ready to leave. Grab a few bits and pieces, just whatever you can carry. I'm going next door to get dressed.'

Dad still lay there staring at him. 'I don't . . . understand . . . where's . . . what's . . .?'

'Dad, there isn't time for this,' Jack interrupted him. 'People are coming here. Bad people. Now MOVE IT!' Dad obeyed instinctively, flailing out of the bed in a tangle of sheets, almost tripping and falling in the process. Jack turned away, hurried to his own room and started taking off his pyjamas, replacing them with jeans and a T-shirt.

'Where's Douglas?' shouted Dad from his room.

'Gone,' said Jack. 'He ratted you out, Dad. He told Giles Hunniford where to find you and then he drove away.'

There was a short silence then. Jack could picture Dad standing frozen in his room in the act of putting on his clothes.

'I don't believe that. Duggie? He wouldn't . . .'

'Keep moving,' Jack advised him. 'We can talk about this later.' He was cramming a spare T-shirt and socks into his rucksack.

'But . . . how do you even know all this?'

'I overheard him,' shouted Jack. It was the only explanation he could think of. 'He . . . he was talking on the phone to Giles Hunniford.'

'What? No way!'

'Way, Dad. Trust me. I was going downstairs to get water and I heard him talking on the phone . . .'

'Well then, why wait till now before . . .?'

'I had to be sure he was gone. In case he turned nasty.'

Dad laughed scornfully. 'Douglas, turn nasty? Are you mad? He would never do anything to—'

'Dad, he's not what you think, OK? He's ratted you out. But there's no time for this!' Jack looked frantically around the room, trying to decide if there was anything else he should take. Not for the first time, he cursed the fact that Dad hadn't allowed them to bring mobile phones with them. A phone would have allowed them to call somebody for help. He thought now about the way that Douglas had ensured that nobody else knew he and Dad were out here. He hadn't been worried about their welfare. He was simply making sure there wouldn't be anybody who could help them.

He remembered the landline down in the sitting room. Maybe he could make a 999 call from that. Maybe . . .

He started as something hit his windowpane with enough force, this time, to crack the glass. Philbert was standing in the back garden again, looking frantic and pointing around the side of the house. Jack swallowed a curse. He opened the window and leaned out into the chill night air.

'Somebody's coming,' hissed Philbert. 'I can see headlights on the road less than a mile away. You need to get out of there now!'

'But . . . it might not be . . .'

'Who else would be driving out here at night? Head for the woods, boy. I'll find you.' Then Philbert turned and lumbered away around the side of the house. Jack ducked back inside and turning, he saw Dad standing in his doorway, dressed now and looking totally bewildered.

'What's going on?' he muttered. 'Who were you talking to?'

'Nobody,' Jack assured him. 'We've got to go now. Somebody's coming.'

Dad stared at him. 'But how do you know that?'

'I saw headlights,' said Jack. 'From the window. We really have to go.' He went to Dad and actually pushed him towards the staircase.

'But . . . you're saying that Duggie is responsible for this? Where is he now?'

'I don't know, Dad. He drove away ten minutes ago. I . . . heard him leave.' They were stumbling down the stairs now, Jack pushing Dad ahead of him.

'Why would he . . .?'

'He must have made some kind of deal. He was talking about money. You know Douglas, he has gambling debts, right?'

'Yes, but he'd never . . . surely, he wouldn't . . .'

'Dad, I'm sorry, but he would. He *has*.' They got to the bottom of the staircase and Jack hesitated, looked hopefully towards the front room, wondering if he still had time to make that call. He ran straight to the phone, lifted the receiver to his ear and registered instantly that there was no dialling tone. He looked down at the phone in dismay and somehow wasn't in the least bit surprised to see that somebody had cut right through the cable. He cursed and told himself that he couldn't afford to panic, that he had to try and stay as cool as possible.

Jack pushed past Dad, shouldering his rucksack as they went. He ran out into the night, heading straight along the lane, with Dad stumbling along behind him. They got to the road and Jack paused to peer to his left. Sure enough, he could see a halo of light appearing over the brow of the hill. For an instant, he froze, mesmerised. Then a dark vehicle, what looked like a four-wheel drive, came into view, travelling fast. As it came downhill, the headlights suddenly went off.

'Come on,' said Jack. He led the way across the road, running for all he was worth. Dad followed. 'Hurry!' yelled Jack.

They ran through the field, the dry lengths of corn whipping at their legs as they blundered through it. 'Where are we going?' yelled Dad.

Jack didn't bother to answer. He'd just noticed that Philbert was in his customary position up ahead, his arms outstretched, his face gazing blankly ahead. *What was he playing at?* Jack glanced over his shoulder and saw to his horror that a dark figure, dressed in what looked like military fatigues, was clambering expertly over the gate, not even pausing to work out how to open it. An instant later, a second man followed. They put their heads down and began to run in pursuit, racing across the field like two dark shadows.

Jack looked imploringly at Philbert as he drew closer. 'Are you just going to stand there?' he yelled.

'I'm going as fast as I can!' replied Dad, misunderstanding.

Philbert didn't move a muscle but as Jack ran past him, he distinctly heard the scarecrow hiss the words, 'Keep running, I'll find ye!'

Jack muttered a curse and kept going. He glanced over his shoulder and saw that Dad, unused to physical exercise, was already dropping behind, while the closer of the two pursuers was rapidly narrowing the distance between them.

'Dad, you have to hurry!' yelled Jack.

'I . . . can't . . .' gasped Dad. 'I'm . . . out of breath . . .'

'You've got to!'

'I . . . Jack you go on . . .'

Just then there was a loud grunt, the sound of an impact. Jack stopped running and turned back to see that Dad had just been felled by a rugby tackle and was lying face down on the ground, while the other man, a big, shaven-headed thug in a camouflage jacket was kneeling on his back and securing Dad's hands with what looked like cable ties. Meanwhile, the second man hadn't slowed his pace at all. Jack stood for a moment in a fog of indecision and actually started to go back but Dad somehow twisted his head to one side and yelled at him. 'Don't stop, Jack! Keep going. Keep—'

The attacker's gloved fist came down in a savage punch, connecting with the side of Dad's face and silencing him. Jack felt the punch, almost as though it had hit him too, but it galvanised him into action, twisting him round and sending him racing on his way again, fear pulsing through him like a shot of pure adrenalin. Perhaps if he could get away, he could find help . . .

He neared the wall on the far side of the field but as he did so he was aware of heavy feet thudding on the ground just behind him. He threw himself forward, vaulted the wall and came down feet first onto the verge of the soft ground that edged the forest. He was aware of his pursuer clambering onto the wall right behind him and grabbing the strap of his rucksack. Jack shrugged himself free of it, spun instinctively around and launched a punch full in to the man's face. He felt something crunch under his knuckles and the man tipped backwards with a howl of pain and dropped out of sight.

Jack twisted away and launched himself at the nearest opening in the dark wall of forest. He ducked under overhanging foliage and ran along a narrow trail, straining to see properly in the moonlight – and once again he was back in the dream he'd had, pursued by some unseen terror. Sure enough, after a few moments, he was aware of sounds coming: something crashing its way through the undergrowth, so he switched to another trail off to his left and then back to one on his right and he kept doing that, moving deeper and deeper into cover.

After a little while, the sounds of pursuit seemed to recede until eventually he couldn't hear them at all and finally, his heart hammering in his chest, his breath exploding from him in hoarse gasps, he spotted a low opening under some bushes and flung himself into their cover. He hugged the ground and twisted round to look back the way he had come, watching the trail along which he had just run, but nobody appeared on it. He made an effort to steady his breathing.

Somewhere an owl hooted, but then a stillness descended and he told himself that, for the moment at least, he had eluded his pursuer – but he didn't have the first idea what he might do next, where he might go for help. He could only hope that Dad was OK, that the two strangers hadn't hurt him any more than that one brutal punch. And for the first time in ages he thought about his mum, off somewhere, living her new life, completely oblivious to the fact that her son was in danger. He wished he could call her and tell her what was going on . . .

He lay for what seemed like hours, afraid to move from his hiding place in case somebody was out there watching – and then his heart jolted in his chest as he became aware of sounds from behind him, the slow crunch of feet through fallen leaves and then the stirring of bushes as somebody lifted the canopy of ferns that overhung the place where he lay. He twisted round onto his back and bunched his hands into fists, determined to sell himself dearly if somebody came at him. He could dimly see now that a hulking figure was moving towards him on its hands and knees, but in the uncertain light, he couldn't get a clear picture of the man's face. He steeled himself, pulled back his right arm to launch a punch, telling himself that he would do that and then he would scramble free and start running again. But a voice made him freeze.

'So this is where ye've been hiding! I told you I'd find you, didn't I?'

'Philbert!' gasped Jack – and then he was almost laughing in sheer relief and scrambling around to hug the big, straw-stuffed figure who was kneeling beside him.

CHAPTER SIXTEEN
REGROUP AND RETHINK

They crouched side by side in the cover of the bushes, staring back down the dark moonlit track along which Jack had recently run. They'd been watching for some time now and there was no sign of anybody following, but Jack wanted to be absolutely sure.

'I'm telling you,' insisted Philbert. 'You're all right for the moment. There's nobody out there. We're wasting time here.'

'But what if they come after me again?' asked Jack.

'They'll be occupied for a wee while. They carried your father back to the lodge. The big laddie had him thrown over one shoulder. He was out cold. The other feller, the smaller one, was furious with you. I'd say you broke his nose.'

'I didn't mean to,' said Jack, looking ruefully at his still-bloody knuckles. 'I was scared and I just kind of . . . lashed out.'

Philbert chuckled. 'Wish I'd seen it,' he said. 'But annoyingly, I was still facing the other way.'

Jack glared at him. 'Yes, so I noticed. Why didn't you help us?'

'What, and tip them off to the fact that you're not on your own?' Philbert sneered. 'That would have been a really stupid move. This has to be played the clever way. This way, I get to listen in, don't I? I get to observe. Nobody thinks twice about blabbing in front of a lump of straw. How do you suppose I learned that your red-faced pal was a wrong 'un in the first place?'

'His name's Douglas,' snapped Jack. 'And he's no pal of mine, not any more. He ratted out Dad, his oldest friend.' He felt that Philbert was trying to change the subject and rounded on him. 'Look, I know you warned us that they were coming and everything but . . . you could see we were in trouble and you just stood there. Would it have killed you to help us?'

Philbert shook his head and his wide-brimmed hat stirred the vegetation overhead. 'You didn't understand, boy. I'm your secret weapon. You need to keep me as a last resort. Like I said, I can listen in on them. I can find out things.'

Jack frowned, unconvinced. 'Oh yeah? So what did you learn that was so helpful?' he asked.

'Well, quite a bit. First of all, the big laddie was pulling the other feller's leg about that broken nose. "Fancy a wee boy getting the better of you!" he said. The other one, who I would say is the nastier of the two, he said something about you catching him unexpectedly, just as he was coming over the wall. He also said . . .'

'Yes?' prompted Jack.

'He also said he would make you very sorry for that punch, when he finally caught up with you.'

Jack let out a slow breath. 'Oh, that's great,' he murmured.

'I wouldn't worry. We're not going to let him catch you, are we?'

'I'm not so sure, for all the help you've been. What else was said?'

'Well, then, the big laddie – the other feller called him Vincent – he said that they'd get your father back inside and then they'd wait for "the contact" to show up with the papers.'

'What does that mean?' asked Jack. 'What contact? What papers?'

'I'm not entirely sure,' admitted Philbert. 'But then Frank, the shorter one, he said, "What if he won't sign?" and Vincent said, "Oh, he'll sign, don't you worry about that."

And then he asked Frank, "What about the kid?" and Frank said, "I'll go out after him as soon as I've put something on my nose. There'll be some time before the contact gets here." And Vincent laughed at that and said, "Are you sure you'll be able to handle the kid all by yourself?" and Frank said . . .' Philbert made a face. 'Well, I don't want to repeat what he actually said, but it was along the lines of Vincent sticking a certain part of his anatomy into another part of his anatomy, which struck me as impossible, unless he was some kind of a contortionist.'

Jack nodded. 'OK, so it sounds like Dad is safe, at least for the time being, at least until this . . . contact arrives. I wonder what's in those papers.'

Philbert shrugged. 'That's anybody's guess,' he said. 'But one thing we do know: Frank will be coming looking for you pretty soon. So we need to be ready for him, don't we?'

'Ready for him, how?' asked Jack nervously.

'Here, come with me; I want to show you something.' Philbert crawled out from cover and Jack reluctantly followed, but he kept throwing nervous glances along the moonlit track behind them, worried that he might see somebody coming in pursuit.

'Will you for pity's sake relax?' Philbert chided him. 'I've already explained, it's going to take him a wee bit of time to find you. Now, follow me.' Philbert started shambling away along another trail and Jack fell obediently into step behind him. As they walked through the darkness, he kept looking to either side of the trail and quickly realised that, left to his own devices, he would be hopelessly lost. Everything looked exactly the same – the tall grey trunks of trees rearing up on all sides, a multitude of twisting tracks leading off at every point of the compass. Even after walking for just another few minutes, Jack no longer had any idea of which direction they had come from. Philbert, though, seemed to know exactly where he was going. He strolled along with ease, turning here and there along different trails as though he was right at home.

'How did you find me?' asked Jack, after they'd walked some distance. 'I mean, I could have been hiding anywhere in this lot.'

'I used this,' said Philbert, tapping the area of sacking where his nose ought to have been. 'You see, I've got a very highly developed sense of smell and you people . . . well, don't take this the wrong way, pal, but you do have your own particular pong.'

Jack was about to reply but Philbert was pointing to something up ahead.

'Ah now, here's what I wanted to show you,' he said.

They had come to a steep and narrow downhill stretch, overhung by low bushes. Jack saw that something brown was hanging from a tree by a length of rope and, as they moved closer, he could just make out that it was a large rabbit, suspended by its back legs. The sound of approaching footsteps seemed to startle it and it began to kick frantically, but Philbert went to it, enveloped it in his stick hands and unhooked its back legs from the length of rope. Then he hugged its quivering shape up against his chest.

'There, there,' he murmured. 'Don't you fret, wee feller.' He turned to look at Jack and waved a hand at the dangling rope. 'This is a very simple snare,' he explained. He pulled on it and showed how the far end of it was attached to a bendy length of willow. He indicated the narrow trail that ran past the tree. 'Here's how it works,' he said. 'The rabbit runs through here, he stands in a noose which triggers the snare and the rope takes him away up into the trees, where he hangs about until I come along.'

Jack stared up at the end of the tree. 'Who put it here?' he asked.

'I did, you numpty. Who do you think? Well, I'm fond of rabbits and they move too quickly for me to catch them by any other means.'

'But why do you . . .?' Jack broke off. Philbert was looking at the quivering rabbit in his grasp and running the tip of his tongue along his lips as he stroked its fur. 'Oh, no, you wouldn't, would you?'

'Of course I would! Rabbit is delicious. Until you've eaten one, you've no idea how tasty it can be.'

'No,' said Jack, decisively, stepping forward. 'No, I'm not standing here and watching you eat a rabbit. I'm sorry, but there have to be some limits.' He reached out, pulled the creature from Philbert's grasp and threw it to the ground. It raced away in an instant, flashing the tuft of its tail in alarm, and was lost in darkness within seconds. Philbert stared after it in dismay. 'Aww, now, that's not fair!' he protested. 'I was looking forward to that!'

'Never mind, there'll be plenty of other chances when I'm not with you,' Jack told him. 'And we've got other things to worry about right now.' He pointed to the length of rope swinging from the end of the sapling. 'Just explain to me exactly how this is going to help?' he said.

Philbert sighed. 'I was going to propose that we set a snare to catch Frank,' he said.

'Surely that would never work,' protested Jack. 'He's a full-grown man!'

'Not *this* kind of snare,' said Philbert. 'Obviously. It wouldn't be able to lift him clear of the ground. But the principle would be the same. And this is the ideal place to do it. You can lead him along this track where I'll be waiting for him under cover. I'll jump on him and knock him out. We'll tie his hands and feet and leave him here. Then we'll only have the one man to worry about.'

'What about this contact they mentioned?' asked Jack, unconvinced.

'Maybe we'll get to Vincent before the contact turns up.'

'And maybe we won't.' Jack frowned. 'It sounds risky, to me. And . . . what if I get him here and you decide to just stand there like a big lump again?'

'I wouldn't do that!'

'You did before.'

'That was different. I was in full view. If anybody had seen me move so much as a muscle, they'd have known there was something different about me. And that you had some help. But out here in the woods, there's nobody to see what we get up to. We'll have him all to ourselves.'

Jack shook his head. 'I don't know,' he murmured. 'What if you decide to leave me to it again? I'd be on my own with him . . . and he's already mad at me.'

'Don't you worry about that, just bring him along and I'll take care of everything. But . . .' He looked at Jack doubtfully. 'This is very important. You'll have to play your part in this or it isn't going to work. I need you to lure him into our trap. And we need him not to think about being ambushed, which means you'll have to stay just one step ahead of him, the whole time.'

Jack frowned. The more he heard about this idea, the less he liked it. 'But why should we need to do all this anyway?' he reasoned. 'Surely, I could find my way to a police station, and tell *them* what's happening?' He considered for a moment and began to warm to the idea. 'Yeah, that would work. I could bring a whole bunch of them back to the house; we could let *them* sort it out. Surely that makes much more sense?' He looked intently at Philbert. 'Where *is* the nearest police station?'

Philbert shrugged his massive shoulders. 'I honestly don't know,' he said.

'You . . . don't know?' Jack glared at him. 'You must do!'

'Why would I? I've never had any dealings with the police. I'm pretty sure there aren't any nearby, so I suppose if you wanted some, you'd have to go to a town or something. I believe I heard Ken tell a visitor that Pitlochry is the nearest one of any size, but . . . well, I can't help you with that neither.'

'Why not?

Philbert spread out his straw-stuffed arms. 'Because all I know is this wood and the fields and the buildings around it. I've never *been* anywhere else.' He looked thoughtful. 'And I can't go walking into a town, can I? People would go crazy! They'd think they were dreaming!'

'Surely we could . . .'

'No. If you go into a town ye'll be on your own. But it occurs to me that time is surely of the essence here? And after all is said and done, it *is* only two men we have to worry about. If we can snare Frank, that only leaves Vincent. Surely you and I could take care of him and then you could get your father away to safety? I mean, how hard can it be?'

Jack licked his lips nervously. 'All right,' he said. 'Here's another idea. What about I head up to the farm and wake up Ken? He's got a phone, he could call the police.'

Philbert's rumpled features arranged themselves into a frown. 'I'm not involving the McFarlanes,' he said. 'I'm supposed to protect them, not put them in harm's way. Those men who've come, you know they have guns?'

Jack swallowed. 'Really?' he murmured.

'Oh aye. When Vincent was carrying your father, I saw a pistol in a holster on his hip.'

Jack considered what Philbert was saying. He was clearly adamant that he wasn't going to endanger Ken and Rhona, and Jack seriously doubted that he could even find his own way to the farm from here without Philbert's help. Meanwhile, he was horribly aware that time was ticking away and that any minute now, Frank might come looking for him. The thought of facing up to the man whose nose he had broken, without some plan of action, was not an appealing one. He realised that he had to make a decision now and he could only hope against hope that it was the right one.

'All right,' he murmured. 'I guess we'll try it your way. So . . . explain to me again. How is this thing going to work?'

CHAPTER SEVENTEEN
THE TRAP

The full moon shone down through the overhead foliage, dappling the ground with moving patterns of light. Soft winds stirred the branches, making the canopy of leaves rustle. Jack glanced at his watch and saw that it was a little after two a.m. He sat on a fallen tree in the middle of the small clearing that Philbert had chosen and waited anxiously. Philbert had left him ten minutes ago, after announcing that his nose was beginning to pick up traces of an approaching man. His last words to Jack had been simple: 'Make sure you bring him along the right trail.'

Jack told himself that this should be pretty foolproof – but he couldn't help remembering how Philbert had stood stock-still earlier when Jack and Dad really needed his help. What if he didn't spring out from hiding as he had promised? What if he stayed hidden in the bushes? Jack would be left alone with the scary man whose nose he had broken.

Jack would be at his mercy, ready to be punched, kicked, maybe even worse . . .

He shook his head, tried to rid himself of such thoughts. He wondered what Dad's state of mind was right now. He hoped that Frank and Vincent hadn't hurt him too much. He kept seeing the recurring image of Vincent's fist coming down to connect with the side of Dad's face, knocking him unconscious. Not for the first time, it occurred to Jack why all this was happening: *because Dad had told the truth about something*! It was unbelievable. When Jack was a little boy, he'd been taught, like most kids he knew, that you should always tell the truth about everything that you saw or heard. But something awful seemed to have happened to the world. Something inexplicable. Now, people were encouraged to either lie about things or to look the other way, even when they knew full well that something bad was going down. Douglas, Dad's best friend, had lied to Dad, assured him that everything would be fine, but behind his back, he'd made a secret deal to give him up to his enemies.

It was horrible and there didn't seem to be any way back from it. Jack hoped that he'd see Douglas again, just so he could tell him how much he despised him for what he'd done.

A soft sound made Jack turn his head and he saw to his horror that a figure was emerging stealthily from the cover of the trees on the far side of the clearing, a short, stocky man in camouflage clothing. It was impossible to be sure in the semi-darkness but Jack knew that it had to be Frank. Jack's first instinct was to get up and run, but Philbert had told him that he had to sit right where he was until Frank was almost upon him.

'Pretend you haven't spotted him,' the scarecrow had said. 'Wait until he's real close, so when you do run, he'll follow you along the right trail without a second thought. You need to be just one step ahead of him the whole time. That way he'll be too intent on you to notice that he's running into a trap.'

It took every ounce of effort Jack possessed to pretend that he hadn't seen Frank. He turned his head aside and pretended to scan the trees to the right of where the man stood. Out of the corner of his eye, he was horribly aware of Frank hunkering down, moving furtively closer, zig-zagging from bush to tree to shrub, attempting to stay under cover as he edged nearer and nearer to his quarry. Jack's heart was pounding in his chest, his hands were trembling, but he made himself sit where he was until Frank was maybe ten metres away. Then, and only then, did he allow himself to look in the man's direction and react, jumping to his feet and beginning to run, heading along the trail that Philbert had picked earlier.

Frank sprang in pursuit and it was clear straight away he was well used to running – he quickly began to close the gap between the two of them, and Jack promptly dispensed with his original notion of running a little more slowly than he was capable of in order to keep the man close on his heels – if he wasn't careful he'd be caught before he even got to the trap!

By the time Jack reached the far side of the clearing, Frank was only a few steps behind him and still closing the gap. Jack's heart hammered in his chest like a drum. Ahead of him, he spotted the narrow trail along which he was supposed to run, the opening barely wide enough to contain him. He ducked his head slightly to avoid banging it on the overhanging bushes and sprinted into the opening, almost overbalancing as the trail plunged steeply downhill, the slope littered with a treacherous mat of fallen leaves. Now he was entering the place where Philbert was supposed to be hiding but as he came alongside the screen of bushes, there was no sign of the scarecrow.

Turning his head to look had caused Jack to take his gaze momentarily off the way ahead. The toe of one sneaker slammed into a tree root and he tripped, pitching face-forward onto the ground, the impact slamming the breath out of him. He slid to the bottom of the incline and struggled around onto his back. Frank had slowed to a walk now and was coming down the slope towards Jack, a malevolent smile on his battered face.

'Oh dear,' he croaked. 'Looks like you tripped up, sunshine.' His damaged nose made it sound like he was suffering from the effects of a particularly bad cold. 'Now, boy, I think it's time you and me had a little talk.'

Jack scrambled upright and stood there in a fog of indecision, looking frantically around for Philbert, but there was no sign of him and Jack experienced a terrible sinking feeling in the pit of his stomach. Philbert had abandoned him again! He told himself that he needed to start running – but even as he thought it, Frank was lifting a hand to prod at his shattered nose. 'Think you're a hard man, don't you?' he murmured. 'Think you can get away with punching me, just because you're only a kid. But I don't let anyone get away with laying a hand on me, doesn't matter how old they are. I'm supposed to take you back to the lodge, but that don't mean I ain't gonna get my own back first.'

Jack held up his hands, telling himself that he mustn't panic. 'You . . . you were chasing me,' he protested. 'I only hit you in self-defence!'

'Is that right?' Frank chuckled. 'Oh don't worry, kid, I ain't gonna kill ya. Not yet, anyway. But I am gonna make you sorry for what you done.' He reached into his camouflage jacket and when his gloved hand emerged it was clutching a large, jagged-bladed knife. 'You should've kept running,' he said.

Jack shook his head. 'But I . . . I wanted to bring you here,' he said.

'Oh yeah. Why's that?'

'I wanted you to meet somebody.' Jack was glancing desperately around. He raised his voice almost to a shout. 'I wanted you to meet a friend of mine!'

Frank grinned mirthlessly. 'What *friend*?' he sneered. He looked slowly around. 'Looks like you're all on your own.'

'I know he's here somewhere,' insisted Jack. 'Really. He's hiding but he's gonna show himself any minute now, you'll see. And then you'll be sorry.'

Frank chuckled nastily. He was getting very close now.

'Well, where is he?' he asked. 'I don't think you've got a friend.'

'Oh yes he has,' growled a voice and a huge figure reared up out of the bushes directly behind Frank. Philbert was holding a heavy branch in both hands and before Frank even had time to turn around, Philbert brought the thick end of it crashing down onto his head with a sickening thud, hitting him so hard that the end of the branch broke off and went tumbling away. Frank dropped to the ground like a puppet whose strings had been cut, clearly knocked unconscious, the knife falling from his hand. Philbert emerged cautiously from cover. He crouched beside Frank for a moment, inspecting him.

'Out cold,' he said, with a nod of satisfaction.

'You certainly took your time,' murmured Jack. He took a few cautious steps closer. 'He's . . . not dead is he?'

Philbert shook his head. 'Nah,' he said. He didn't sound as though he cared much, either way. 'Just sleepin'. He'll have a big lump on his head, though.'

'You hit him really hard.'

'Aye. Good stuff, eh?' Philbert grinned his rotten grin and rummaged in the bushes until he found the length of rope that he'd used to make the original snare. He turned

Frank over onto his front and started tying his hands securely behind his back.

'What are we going to do with him?' asked Jack.

Philbert shrugged his shoulders. 'We'll leave him in the bushes for now. I'll make a gag, so he can't shout for help. You can tell people about him later.'

'And who will I say knocked him out?'

Philbert frowned. 'You, I suppose.'

Jack shook his head. 'But he's going to know it wasn't me, isn't he?' he protested. 'When he comes round. He was looking straight at me when you hit him from behind.'

'Well, don't worry about it for now. You'll think of something.' Philbert was lifting Frank's legs up at the knees and securing his ankles to his bound wrists, using the same length of rope. 'The main thing is he's out of action until somebody finds him. Now, what about a wee gag?' He reached in the pocket of his jacket and pulled out a dirty old kerchief. 'This should do the job,' he said, and turning Frank onto his side, he started to bind the length of cloth tight around his open mouth.

Just at that moment, there was a loud electronic squelch, which made Jack start. He looked down at Frank in alarm. 'What was that?' he asked, panicked.

'Something in his jacket pocket,' said Philbert, pointing a stick finger.

'Get it out,' suggested Jack. 'It could be a mobile phone.'

Philbert reached into Frank's pocket and pulled out a small square handset. He stood up and brought it over to Jack. It was some kind of a walkie-talkie, Jack decided. He'd seen them in movies, but he'd never actually used one. He noticed that there was a large central button with the word TALK printed on it, so it seemed pretty straightforward. Now an impatient voice spilled out of the speakers, speaking in an urgent whisper.

'Christ sake, Frank, haven't you found the little bleeder yet?'

Jack and Philbert exchanged baffled looks.

A silence. Then again, the weird electronic squelch, before the voice spoke again. 'Frank? Are you there? Come in, for God's sake, you've been ages.'

Jack decided that there was no option but to reply. He pressed the button and remembered to try and make his voice sound deeper. 'Er . . . yeah, I got him,' he growled. He released the button.

A puzzled silence. Then; 'Frank, that you? You sound funny.'

Jack scowled, bit his lip, then pressed the button again. 'Yeah. It's . . .' He had a sudden inspiration. He gripped his nose between his thumb and forefinger. 'It's my nose,' he said. 'I fink it's broken.'

'Yeah, I already know that, don't I? But listen, the kid's all right, isn't he? I understand that you'd want to slap him around a bit, but you didn't hurt him too much, did ya?'

'No. No, he's OK.'

'Right, good. Well, you need to get him back here, in one piece, ASAP. Our contact could be here at any minute.'

'Er . . . Roger that.'

'You what?'

'Er . . . on my way.' Jack released the button. He listened for a moment, but there were no further comments, so he thrust the handset into his jacket pocket. He looked up at Philbert. 'What are we supposed to do now?' he asked.

Philbert shrugged. 'I'll hide Frank and then . . .'

'Yes?'

'We . . . go to the lodge?'

'Oh yeah.' Jack gestured at Frank's body. 'Because it's all gone very well, so far, doing it by ourselves, right?'

Philbert frowned. 'I'm getting the distinct impression you're not happy with me,' he said.

'Oh, you really think so?' Jack gestured again at Frank's prostrate body. 'Look, I appreciate you were helping me out there, but . . . well, you could have killed him, hitting him like that!'

'I didn't though, did I? Look, he's still breathing. Besides, I don't know why you're so worried about *him*. What do you think he was going to do with that knife? Whittle you a present?"

'No, course not. But . . .' Jack thought for a moment. 'I suppose if I say we should go to the police now, you'll say you don't know how to find them. Right?'

Philbert nodded. 'That's correct,' he said. 'I'm very sorry.'

'And . . . what if I was to head into the village and try and get some kind of help there?'

'You could do that, certainly. But you'd be on your own if you did. I can't let anyone there see me, either.' Philbert sighed. 'Look,' he said, 'you can waste as much time as you like. But it seems to me that while we're standing here yapping, your father's in trouble and we're the only ones who can help him. Now, I don't much care for the man after some of the things he's said about me, but I expect *you* do, so if I were you, I'd stop making excuses and get back to the lodge and help him.'

Jack shook his head. 'When you put it like that, I guess I don't have much choice,' he said.

'I don't think you do,' agreed Philbert. 'I say, let's go and get the job done.'

'All right. But listen, if you have to hit anybody else . . .'

'Aye?'

'Don't hit them quite so hard, OK?'

Philbert nodded. 'Deal,' he said. He crouched down again and lifted Frank's body into his arms, as though he weighed no more than a doll. He stood up. 'I'll just get rid of this feller,' he said, matter-of-factly.

'Get rid of him?' cried Jack, appalled. 'What do you mean?'

'Relax. I'm just goin' to hide him in yon bushes!' He turned away. 'I'll only be a few minutes. You wait here for me.' He strode away into the undergrowth, using Frank's body to push branches aside as he went. In moments, he was lost from sight and Jack was left alone in the darkness to wonder, once again, if he was doing the right thing.

CHAPTER EIGHTEEN

AN ALTERCATION

They ran through the forest and found themselves looking over the wall and out across Philbert's moonlit field. Beyond the far wall, the downstairs curtains of the lodge were tightly drawn. The porch light was off and there were no signs of life. Dad's car was still parked outside, Jack noticed, but there was no sign of the men's four-wheel drive. 'Maybe Vincent has gone?' whispered Jack, hopefully.

Philbert shook his head. 'I heard him tell Frank they should move their vehicle up the road a bit, so as not to draw too much attention to the house,' said Philbert. 'No, he's in there all right, waiting for Frank to get back with you.'

'So what are we going to do?' asked Jack. 'We can't just walk up and knock on the door, can we?'

'No, of course not. We need to draw him out of there. We need some kind of a diversion. I think the best thing we can do is—' He broke off suddenly as he noticed some-thing on the road beyond the field. 'Oh no,' he said, quietly. 'I wasn't expecting that.'

'What's the matter?' asked Jack. He scanned the scene and then noticed a figure moving along the road on the other side of the far wall, a familiar figure dressed in a heavy padded jacket. Rhona, no doubt out on one of her regular head-clearing walks. 'What's she doing out so early?' murmured Jack.

'Maybe she'll just keep walking,' murmured Philbert hopefully.

But no, now Rhona was slowing to a halt. She was staring over the gate into the field at the abandoned wooden cross. Even at this distance, Jack could sense her outrage. She looked to her left, to her right and then she turned and gazed towards the lodge. She hesitated for just a moment and then started to walk towards it.

'Oh, no,' gasped Jack. 'She's going towards the lodge!' He glanced back but there was suddenly no sign of Philbert. He must have ducked back into the cover of the under-growth. 'Hey!' hissed Jack, 'What are you doing?' But for the moment, at least, there was no answer. Jack tried not to panic. He wasn't sure what to do for the best, but he

did know that he couldn't let Rhona go and ring the doorbell of the lodge. Who knew what might happen to her?
He acted instinctively, without really pausing to think it
through. He placed his forefingers into either side of his
mouth and let out a really loud whistle, something he had
learned to do years ago. It did the trick. Rhona stopped in
her tracks and turned back to gaze into the field. There
was nothing else for it. Jack stepped a few paces out from
cover and waved his arms frantically at her. She saw him
and immediately walked towards the field.

'She's coming!' hissed Jack.

'No,' said Philbert, from his place of concealment. 'No,
she can't do that. I can't let her see me.'

'You're going to have to,' argued Jack.

'No. One piggy is enough!'

'But Philbert, she's . . .' Jack looked doubtfully at Rhona.
She was striding through the corn towards him, and even
at this distance he could sense that she was angry. Jack
stayed where he was, ready to jump back into cover if
anybody should come out of the lodge. Now Rhona had
reached Philbert's cross. She paused for a moment to inspect
it, as though looking for clues, and then she came on again,
swinging her arms by her side, looking like she meant

business. She started talking before she had even reached Jack.

'What the hell are you doing out here at this time of night?' she demanded.

'I could ask you the same thing!' retorted Jack.

'I couldn't sleep. I came out to clear my head.' She waved a hand, dismissing the question. 'Where's Philbert? What have you done with him?'

He held up his hands to placate her. 'Don't worry, he's fine,' he assured her. 'Really.' He pointed towards the forest. 'I've got him stashed away in there, safe and sound.'

'But why move him? The crows will be at the corn as soon as the sun comes up. If this is your idea of a joke, I don't think it's very funny.'

'It's no joke, I promise you. Listen, Rhona, there's something I need to tell you about Philbert—'

'He's not just any old scarecrow, you know. He's special.'

'Er . . . yes, that's exactly what I'm trying to—'

'So you'd better not have damaged him.'

'I haven't. He's OK. He's just a bit . . . er . . . shy.'

'*Shy*?' Her eyes narrowed suspiciously. 'What are you talking about?'

He sighed. He turned and looked towards the trees. 'You'd better come out now,' he said. 'Let's get it over with.'

Rhona had finally reached Jack. She came to a halt and stood there beside him, her hands on her hips. She still looked annoyed. 'Who are you talking to?' she asked him.

'To . . . Philbert,' he said, and now she looked furious.

'Yes, very funny,' she said. She gave him a sarcastic slow handclap. 'But we need to put him back before the sun comes up. And you haven't answered my question. Why did you move him?'

'I didn't. He walked. He . . . does that.' Again, he turned to look towards the trees. 'Come on, Philbert, you *have* to show her.'

Silence.

'Look, Jack,' said Rhona, 'I don't know what's going on here, but I've a good mind to go and tell your dad that you've been messing around with . . .'

'No, you can't do that!' Jack took a step closer. 'You have to promise me you'll stay away from the lodge, whatever you do. Listen, Rhona, this is probably going to sound crazy . . .'

'Oh, you think so?'

'. . . But right now, Dad's being held prisoner in there

212

by this guy who was sent from London to get him. He's got a gun. There were two guys, actually, but one of them . . . well, we managed to knock him out and tie him up. He's hidden in the woods. But the other one is still in the lodge, so, please stay out of it until me and Philbert have had a chance to sort things out.'

Rhona looked at him in silence for a few moments. 'Are you on something?' she asked him.

'What do you mean?' he asked her. 'Like what?'

'I don't know. Drugs? Because, I have to tell you, you are talking like a crazy person.'

'Yeah, I know it sounds a bit weird, of course it does, but . . . look, you have to trust me, OK? You can do that, can't you?' He turned back to the bushes. 'Philbert, I mean it. You are going to have to come out of there and show yourself. I'm starting to look a bit stupid here.' There was no reply. 'Philbert?' he repeated. 'Show yourself. *Please!*'

'I've had enough of this,' said Rhona. She pushed Jack roughly aside and stepped past him into the bushes. Jack waited, hardly daring to breathe. There was a long silence and then he heard Rhona say, 'Oh my God!'

'Yes!' whispered Jack. He hurried after her into the

undergrowth and found her kneeling beside Philbert's prostrate form. He was lying on his back, staring blankly up at the foliage above him, his arms extended on either side of him. Rhona turned to glare at Jack. 'Why did you put him here?' she cried.

'I didn't,' protested Jack.

'Oh, right, so I suppose he walked over here by himself, did he?'

'Well, yes, I mean . . .' Jack threw himself onto his knees beside her. He glared into Philbert's expressionless eyes. 'You're making me look like an idiot here,' he said. 'Will you *please*, just say something? A simple "hello" will do!'

Rhona looked at Jack pityingly. 'You don't know when to stop, do you?' she said. 'I mean, Jesus! I thought you were nice, but I'm really beginning to wonder.' She leaned down and hooked her arms around the scarecrow. 'Here, at least give me a hand to get him back into the field.'

'You won't be able to budge him,' said Jack. 'He's really heavy.'

'He's made of bloody straw!' cried Rhona and she stood upright, easily lifting Philbert in her arms.

'No,' said Jack. 'No, you can't . . . because he's . . .' He got to his feet and took hold of Philbert's shoulders

– and he realised that she was right. He weighed hardly anything.

'Come on,' she said and started back towards the field, the two of them carrying Philbert between them. Jack began to harangue the scarecrow as they walked, desperate now to provoke some kind of reaction. 'Can't you see how this makes me look?' he implored. 'I'm like some kind of nut-job here.' No reaction. 'Look, I appreciate all the help you've given me so far, I really do, but I need you to do this one last thing for me. I mean, how hard can it be to admit to somebody else that you're alive?' There was still no answer. 'I swear Philbert, if you don't speak or move by the time I count to five, I'm having nothing more to do with you!'

'Something I'm sure he'll be very grateful for,' murmured Rhona. 'Look, are you sure you're OK? Is there something you need?'

He gave her a wounded look. 'Like what?' he asked her.

'I don't know. Didn't your dad say something once about medication?'

The question hit Jack like a punch to the chest. He looked at her and then he looked at the lifeless straw figure in his arms and it finally came to him that perhaps Rhona was absolutely right. Philbert really was nothing more than some old clothes stuffed with straw. Could it be . . . could it *really* be that Jack had imagined it all – everything that Philbert said and did? After all, who else had witnessed what Jack had? Only Frank, he thought, but he was in no position to say anything, because he was tied up and hidden in the forest . . .

'No,' he said. 'Philbert, tell her!' He lifted a hand and began to prod his index finger into Philbert's stomach, remembering how the scarecrow had complained that it hurt him. 'You can feel that, can't you? Eh? Does that hurt, Philbert? Answer me! Say something!"

Rhona lifted a hand and pushed Jack hard in the chest, nearly knocking him over. 'Get away from him!' she cried. 'What are you trying to do?'

They had reached the empty cross now, and she lifted Philbert gently, almost tenderly, into position against it. She began securing his outstretched arms with the lengths of dangling rope. 'I want you to stay out of this field from now on,' she told Jack. 'Do you hear me? I don't want you coming anywhere near him after this.'

Jack shook his head. His eyes were filling with tears. 'You don't understand,' he pleaded with her. 'I . . . *saw* him. He *talked* to me. I know he did.'

She looked at him defiantly for a moment and then the hostile expression in her eyes softened. 'Look,' she said, 'I'm worried about you, Jack. I don't know what that medication is for but it seems to me that maybe you've missed taking a couple of doses. Is that it?'

Jack looked at his feet. 'M-maybe,' he whispered.

'I think I *will* have a quick word with your dad,' she said. She turned and started walking towards the wall, but Jack had hardly even registered her words, because now other thoughts were crowding in on him, terrible thoughts. If he'd imagined Philbert, maybe he'd imagined other things. The two camouflage-jacketed men who had come after Dad in the black four-wheel drive . . . The fight with Frank in the woods . . . What if none of it was true? Rhona was right: he hadn't been taking his meds, he'd deliberately stopped after the first day. Could that be it? His hallucinations had come back, but a thousand times more vivid than before? And everything he thought he'd seen had just been a series of crazy images conjured up in his head?

He looked again at Philbert but his face was expressionless, staring straight ahead. It was ridiculous to even think that rumpled, stained old piece of sacking could ever have been alive.

Jack realised in the middle of his thoughts that Rhona was no longer standing beside him. He turned and saw that she was already passing through the gateway of the field. And then he had a wave of doubt. Could he really have imagined those two shaven-headed men? And whatever else had happened, Douglas definitely had driven away in the middle of the night . . .

'Hang on,' he murmured. 'No!' He came to his senses and began to run after Rhona, waving his arms. 'Wait!' he yelled. 'Rhona, wait!'

She turned to look back at him, with an expression of deep irritation. She shrugged her shoulders and turned away again, began to cross the road. 'Rhona!' he yelled. He flung himself across the intervening space and pushed through the gate, but she was already striding up the drive towards the lodge. He caught up with her halfway there and grabbed her arm. He tried to pull her back towards the road but she resisted.

'Let go of me!' she said.

'Rhona, please,' he begged her. 'You can't go to the door. You have to come with me now!'

She shook him off. 'Don't be ridiculous. I just want a quick word with your dad, that's all.'

'He . . . he can't come to the door. I already told you, he's being held prisoner. Please, Rhona, you can't ring that doorbell!'

'Get off me! What's the matter with you?'

'I'm trying to explain. There's something bad happening in there. You . . .'

He broke off as the front door swung open. Vincent came out and stood on the doorstep. Jack saw, to his horror, that he was holding one of Douglas's shotguns. He looked at the two of them with a mirthless smile.

'Well, well,' he said. 'Visitors. You should have let me know you were coming, I'd have baked a cake.' He waved the gun at them. 'You'd better come in,' he said, and stood aside to let them pass.

CHAPTER NINETEEN
SIEGE

They stepped into the living room and Vincent shut the door behind him. The only light in there came from a small table lamp in the corner. Dad was slumped on the sofa, his hands still tied behind his back. One side of his face was badly bruised from the punch he'd received earlier that night. He looked up at Jack and Rhona as they came in and his face fell. 'I hoped you'd got away,' he murmured. He looked so crushed that Jack felt compelled to go straight to him and give him a hug. Rhona just stood there, her eyes wide, gazing from Jack and Dad across to Vincent, who was standing there holding the gun, his face expressionless. It was clearly just beginning to dawn on her that Jack had been telling her the truth, at least about this part of his story.

Vincent stepped forward and prodded the barrel of his gun between Jack's shoulder blades. 'Step away,' he said,

220

his voice flat and calm. Like Frank, he had a London accent. Jack froze for a moment, then did as he was told, keeping his hands where Vincent could see them. Vincent motioned for him to turn around and sit down beside his father and Jack really didn't feel like disobeying.

'Look,' said Dad, leaning forward. 'They're just kids. They've got nothing to do with any of this. Surely you can let them go?'

Vincent ignored the comment. He glanced at Rhona and pointed to the empty armchair. 'You,' he snapped. 'Sit there and keep quiet.' When Rhona hesitated, he added, 'Move it!' She did as she'd been told and sat there looking fearfully back at him. 'Mobile phone,' he added, gesturing with his free hand.

Rhona looked at him blankly.

'Your mobile!' he said, more urgently this time. She reached reluctantly into the pocket of her overalls, pulled out her iPhone and handed it to him. He gave it a cursory glance, then dropped it onto the stone hearth of the fireplace and crushed it beneath the heel of his boot. It made a horrible splintering sound as it shattered.

'Hey!' Rhona started to get up from her seat, but Vincent prodded her in the chest with the shotgun and she dropped obediently back into position. 'When I tell you to do something, you do it,' he said. 'Understand?' Now Vincent looked expectantly at Jack. 'Mobile,' he said.

Jack shook his head. 'Haven't got one,' he muttered.

Vincent sneered. 'Yeah, pull the other one. A teenager without a phone? Not very likely, is it?'

'It's true,' Dad assured him. 'We didn't bring our mobiles with us. Jack wanted to, but I wouldn't let him. I thought they'd be too easy to trace.'

Vincent seemed to consider this for a moment. He gave Jack an intense stare. 'You'd better be telling me the truth,' he said. 'If I find out you're lying to me, you won't like the consequences.' He seemed puzzled. 'So . . . where's Frank?' he asked.

Jack scowled, decided to play dumb. 'Who?'

'Frank. My partner.'

Jack shrugged his shoulders. 'No idea,' he said, and he was glad this was more or less true. It made it easier to face up to Vincent's menacing gaze.

'You expect me to believe that? I happen to know he found you. He *told* me he had. Said he was bringing you straight back here. And then you turn up without him. What's going on?'

It was a very good question, one that Jack didn't have the first idea how to answer. What *was* happening? His head was virtually bursting with questions he couldn't answer. The man called Frank was lying tied up and unconscious in the forest, he was sure of that, but exactly what had happened to him? It had seemed to Jack at the time that Philbert had clubbed him to the ground, but now he wasn't even sure that Philbert was real. What if he *was* just a figment of Jack's imagination? If that was the case, there was only one other person who could possibly have attacked Frank . . . and whatever else happened, he couldn't let Vincent come to that conclusion.

'I haven't seen anyone,' insisted Jack, desperately trying to keep his expression blank. 'I . . . came back because I was worried about my dad.'

Vincent scowled. He reached into his pocket and pulled out a walkie-talkie. Before Jack even had time to think about it, Vincent pressed the button on the handset – and a loud electronic squawk issued from Jack's pocket.

Vincent glared at Jack in silence for a moment. Then he stepped forward and thrust a hand into his jacket. He pulled out the handset and looked at it in disbelief. 'Where did you get this?' he demanded.

Jack told himself not to panic. 'I . . . er . . . f-found that in the woods,' he said. 'It was just . . . lying there.'

Vincent took a threatening step closer. 'I thought I told you not to lie to me,' he snarled. 'Now I'll ask you one more time, where did you get it?'

Jack shook his head. It was beginning to dawn on him that he and his dad, and Rhona too, were in terrible trouble here. Nobody else knew what was going on. They were all at Vincent's mercy. He could kill them and nobody would know a thing about it. His only hope was to play for time . . .

'I . . . already told you,' he stammered. 'It was just lying there . . . in the middle of the woods. So I . . . I picked it up and put it in my pocket. I wasn't even sure what it was.'

Vincent snorted derisively. 'Oh, so you're saying that Frank just dropped his walkie-talkie, is that it? He just . . . threw it away? Because it was getting too heavy for him?' He shook his head. 'Where is he now? Tell me.'

'I honestly don't know. I . . . haven't seen him since he went past me in the woods.'

'He went past you?'

'Yes, I was hiding in some bushes and that's the last time I saw him.' Jack thought for a moment. 'Maybe . . . maybe we should go and look for him?' he suggested. He was thinking that at least if he could get everybody out of the lodge, they might find some way of escaping. But Vincent wasn't having any of it.

'Nobody's going nowhere,' said Vincent. 'We're just going to sit here nice and quiet, until somebody arrives.'

Jack looked at Dad. 'Who's coming?' he asked.

Dad shrugged. 'He won't tell me. I must have asked a hundred times.'

'Yeah, and I told you if you asked one more time, I'd put a gag on you,' said Vincent. He was looking very edgy now, no doubt wondering what had happened to Frank. Jack sensed that he was worried and was trying not to show it.

Rhona finally found her voice. 'You,' she said. 'You . . .' She pointed to the smashed remains of her phone. 'You'll pay for that. Do you hear me? I had to save up for an entire year to buy that!'

Vincent gave her a weary look. 'Don't start,' he said. 'Not unless you want a good slapping.' He lifted the handset of the walkie-talkie and tapped it against his teeth a couple of times, as though trying to think. Then he set it down on the mantelpiece and pulled a mobile phone from his pocket. He walked to the back of the sofa and dialled a number with the thumb of his right hand, keeping the shotgun held in the crook of his left. He waited a moment and when the call was answered, he spoke, pacing up and down as he did so. 'It's me,' he said. A pause. '*Me!* Well, who do you bloody think it is? I'm not saying my name over the phone, am I?' Another pause. 'Right, Sherlock, well done. Listen up. I need you back here, sharpish.'

There was a long pause and Jack was dimly aware of somebody talking excitedly on the other end of the line.

'I know that wasn't the deal,' said Vincent. 'But it's gone pear-shaped, innit? My friend's disappeared.'

Another pause. More jabbering.

'I'm not saying *his* name either! My assistant. And don't you bloody say it! Christ!' Vincent seemed to be getting angrier by the minute. 'How do I know where he is? He went out after the kid and he hasn't come back.' A pause. 'No, no, I've got the boy now. He just . . . turned up. And some girl that was with him . . .' He broke off at a barrage of shouting at the other end. 'I don't know her name, do I? Some teenager with red hair . . . well, what was I supposed to do? The two of them just arrived at the door. I couldn't let her go, could I?' He scowled, listening for a moment. 'Yeah, look, I don't care *where* you are, if you want your money, you're going to have to turn the car around and come back, because I need another pair of hands on this. Yes, I appreciate it's not your field of expertise, but I can't be expected to do this on my own, can I?'

Vincent listened for a few more moments, shaking his head as the person on the other end of the line talked. 'Enough,' he interrupted. 'End of conversation. Like I said, just get here pronto or the deal's off.'

Vincent ended the call and slipped the phone into his pocket.

'Was that Douglas you were talking to?' asked Jack, intrigued.

Vincent glared at him, then leaned closer and tapped him on the nose. 'Keep this out,' he suggested. 'And you'll do a whole lot better.'

But Jack was pretty sure it *had* been Douglas, because whoever it was had recognised Rhona from Vincent's short description.

There was a long silence then. They all sat in their places while Vincent paced edgily back and forth behind them.

'My son needs to take his medication,' said Dad.

'Oh, is that right?' Vincent gave a derisive laugh. 'Tough.' He looked intently at Jack. 'Tell me again about Frank.'

Jack licked his dry lips. 'There's nothing to tell. I hid where he couldn't find me. He walked on by. I . . . waited a while and then I came back here . . .'

'Rubbish! He talked to me on that.' He pointed to the walkie-talkie on the mantelpiece. 'He said he'd got you and he was on his way back.'

Jack shrugged. 'Maybe . . . maybe he was lying to you. Maybe he didn't like it that a kid could get the better of him. Or . . . maybe he double-crossed you.'

Vincent's eyes dilated. He muttered something under his breath. 'He wouldn't do that. He'll turn up,' he murmured. 'When he realises you came back here. But I don't get why he'd drop the walkie-talkie. That don't make sense.'

There was another simmering, resentful silence. Then Dad spoke. 'So how does this work?' he asked Vincent. 'Giles Hunniford paid you to come out here and get me, right?'

'No comment,' said Vincent.

'And now we have to wait for somebody else to get here. That *was* Douglas on the phone just now, wasn't it? But it's not him we're waiting for. Because, he wasn't expecting to be called. So who else is there?'

Vincent didn't say anything.

'I heard something before about . . . a contact?' said Jack.

Vincent looked at him. 'What do you know about that?' he growled.

'I . . . I heard Frank say something about it. When I was hiding from him.'

'Oh right, he was wandering around the woods, talking to himself, was he?'

'No,' said Jack. 'No, he was speaking to somebody on his mobile. I heard him say something about a . . . a contact.'

Vincent came around from behind the sofa. He crouched down in front of Jack and looked him straight in the eyes. 'When I was a lad,' he said, 'my old man always told me that little boys should be seen and not 'eard. The first time he said it, I didn't really understand. I kept right on yapping, didn't I? Cos, you know, kids are likely to do that, ain't they? So my dad, what he did was, he took me into my bedroom and he took the leather belt from around his waist . . . you know what happened next?'

Jack gazed back at him. 'His . . . pants fell down?' he suggested.

Vincent chuckled then, but there was no humour in it.

'Yeah, see, that's just what I would have said, before he showed me what he meant.' He leaned a little closer. 'Before he put me straight. Shall I tell you what he did?'

'There's no need,' Jack assured him.

'Oh, but I think it's important. See, what happened, he leathered me so hard with that belt that I couldn't sit down for a week without crying.' He smiled mirthlessly. 'Now if you'd like a demonstration of what my old man did to me, you just keep right on talking, OK?'

'Look,' said Dad. 'Please . . . there's no need to get nasty. For God's sake, he's just a kid, he hasn't done anything.'

'Yeah, well you want to teach him not to question his elders and betters.'

Rhona laughed at that. 'Elders and betters?' she cried. 'You're standing there with a gun and you think that makes you better? From where I'm sitting, that makes you a bully.'

Vincent turned his icy gaze upon Rhona.

'As for you,' he said, 'Don't go thinking that you can get away with anything just because you're a girl. A belt don't make no distinction between boys and girls. It's all just flesh to a belt. You'd do well to remember that.' He stood up, walked round the sofa and went back to his pacing.

The time passed with agonising slowness. Jack kept

glancing at his watch to see that only minutes had crept by. It seemed like hours had passed when they finally heard the sound of a car pulling in to the driveway and they saw the glare of headlights through the little glass window in the front door.

'Finally,' murmured Vincent. He went to the door and opened it a little, as though checking that the visitor was the one he was expecting. A man came in, a weasel-faced little fellow in a business suit, carrying a leather briefcase. Jack judged him to be about fifty years old, thin and pasty-looking, with straggles of greying hair combed down flat on his skull. He closed the door behind him and looked quickly around at the occupants of the room. He seemed somewhat surprised when he registered Rhona and looked across at Vincent, who shrugged his shoulders, as if to say that there was nothing he could do about the matter. The man rolled his eyes, but for the moment, said nothing. He walked calmly over to the dining table, placed the briefcase on it, unlatched it and took out a slim folder, which he set down on the table. Then he turned back and gave the three captives an oily smile. He rubbed his hands together.

'Right,' he said. 'We'll get straight down to business, shall we?'

CHAPTER TWENTY

THE DEAL

The man in the suit took one of the wooden chairs from the dining table and placed it in front of Jack and his father. He picked up the slim file, sat himself down and flipped it open. Jack could see that it contained several sheets of typed paper. The man perused the contents for a few moments as though checking a particular detail. He seemed satisfied with what he saw there. He looked up at Dad and smiled, thinly.

'So,' he said. 'What I have here is a document – one that I've had drawn up on your behalf.' He had a refined southern accent. 'Its contents are quite complicated, but essentially it's a confession, which I would like you to sign.'

Dad narrowed his eyes suspiciously.

'A confession?' he echoed. 'A confession to what?'

The man sighed, as though he considered this kind of detail too trivial to bother with, but he explained anyway.

'Obviously you'll want to read through it before you sign,' he said. 'But in basic terms, you will be confessing to the fact that your recent allegations are lies . . . that you made up the list of names which you handed to your employers and which you sent to various other third parties.'

There was a long silence as the truth sank in. Dad spluttered. 'I . . . I can't put my name to that!' he protested. 'I . . . I didn't make anything up. I found the information in the bank's records!'

The man looked annoyed that Dad felt he had to mention this.

'Yes, of course, I understand. It's very hard to have principles in this life and naturally, we all want to live up to the ones we hold dear, that's only human nature. But I'm sure I don't have to tell you that some very powerful people were named on the list you so recklessly gave out – people who would be highly embarrassed to be identified as . . . inside traders. People who are a good deal more influential than you are.' The man tapped the cover of the file with a nicotine-stained index finger. 'This is designed to exonerate them – and the only way we can do that is if you tell the world that you lied about my clients – that you did it out of sheer malice, because you were jealous of their success and wanted to see them brought down. Now, you might say that to put your name to such a document would be making you every bit as corrupt as they are, and I wouldn't argue the point. But I'm afraid you really don't have much choice in the matter. You *will* sign this document, one way or another. We'll make sure of that.'

Dad frowned. He sat there, his head lowered, as though thinking it over. Then he looked up again. 'And what happens if I refuse?' he said.

The man glanced across at Vincent, as though to remind Dad that he was still standing there. 'Let's just say that there are ways to make a man do most things and that my associate over there knows every one of them in all their ghastly detail. What's more, he's perfectly willing to make sure that you comply with my request.'

Dad gasped. 'Are you talking about . . . torture?' he cried.

Jack felt a jolt of fear pulse through him and when he looked at Rhona, he saw the terror in her expression, her eyes wide, her mouth open.

'I didn't say it,' the man told Dad. '*You* did.'

'Yes, but that's what you're getting at, isn't it?'

'I really couldn't say,' said the man. 'My advice would

be not to put the matter to the test. We'll just sign the papers, shall we?'

Jack couldn't restrain himself any longer. 'Who are you?' he asked.

The man turned his head towards Jack and it was like looking into the eyes of something that was already dead. Jack saw no compassion there, no interest of any kind. He might as well be talking to a block of wood.

'It doesn't matter who I am,' said the man. 'I'm . . . a fixer. I get things that have gone wrong fixed. They may not be the most pleasant things in the world, but I am handsomely paid for my efforts and I always carry out my orders to the letter. On this occasion, my orders are very simple. "Get a man to sign a confession." Easy as that.' The Fixer shrugged. 'So . . .' He returned his attention to Dad. 'It's really up to you, old boy. We can do this the easy way or the hard way. Trust me, you really do *not* want to do it the hard way. And let me remind you that it's not just *you* we're talking about. You may be stoic enough to stand pain, I've seen that happen once or twice and I always applaud the bravery of such people, but how would you feel if it were one of these two –' he nodded first towards Jack and then Rhona – 'being punished for something you have done?'

'You . . . you wouldn't do that,' reasoned Dad.

'No, of course I wouldn't,' the Fixer assured him. 'But then, it wouldn't be me doing it. My associate here isn't particularly fussy about who he hurts.' He looked at Vincent. 'Am I correct in that assumption?'

Vincent shrugged his shoulders. 'All the same to me,' he said. 'I'm an equal opportunities sort of person.'

Dad swallowed. He seemed to be thinking furiously. 'All right,' he said. 'Let's say I *do* sign your rotten piece of paper. What happens to us then? Can you guarantee that we'll be allowed to leave here unharmed?'

The Fixer looked almost sad at this question. 'My dear fellow, I can't guarantee you anything,' he said. 'That's really not my department.'

Dad turned his head to look at Vincent, but the man just gazed straight back at him, his expression blank.

Dad shook his head. 'You're not going to let us leave, are you? You know I'd only go straight back to the newspapers and tell them I was made to sign this confession. You can't risk that, can you?'

The Fixer didn't reply. He glanced at his watch as though impatient. 'We're wasting time,' he said.

'Maybe . . . maybe you could promise me that if I signed,

236

nothing would happen to my son here . . . or to Rhona. I mean, come on, help me out here! Neither of them have had anything to do with this. They've done nothing. They're just kids! You surely wouldn't harm *them*, would you? You can't be that evil.'

The Fixer gazed straight back at him. 'Evil is a very strong word,' he said. 'I prefer "efficient".' And I think these two youngsters are what is generally termed "collateral damage". I sympathise, I really do, but you're the one who put them in harm's way when you decided to blow the whistle. You have nobody to blame but yourself. Now, if you really wouldn't mind, I'd appreciate it if we could get this little matter done. I have a long drive ahead of me.'

Dad's eyes filled with tears and Jack felt compelled to put an arm round him. Dad shrugged his shoulders. 'I can't sign with my hands tied,' he gasped.

'Of course not,' said the Fixer. 'We'll untie you. But please, don't be so stupid as to try anything silly.' He nodded to Vincent, who stepped forward, pulling a knife from his belt. Leaning over the back of the sofa, he pushed Dad roughly forward and cut through the cable tie that bound Dad's hands tightly together behind his back. Dad gave a sigh of relief and kneaded his left wrist with his right hand.

He looked at Jack. 'I'm so sorry,' he murmured. 'I never dreamed you'd be involved in this.'

'It's not your fault,' said Jack. 'You haven't done anything wrong.' But he thought again about his mother, and how he wished he'd tried harder to contact her before all this kicked off. It was beginning to feel as though he wouldn't get another chance. He glanced across at Rhona and she sent a steely look back at him, as though trying to assure him that everything would be all right. But he didn't see how it could be now. It felt as though they were all doomed.

'I don't have a pen,' croaked Dad.

The Fixer nodded. He reached into his inside pocket and took out a fancy-looking fountain pen. He leaned forward on his seat and handed the file and the pen to Dad, who took them from him. Vincent stayed at the back of the sofa, the knife still clutched in his right hand, the shotgun cradled in the crook of his left arm, watching carefully in case Dad tried anything. Jack weighed up his options, telling himself that this might be his last chance to try and do something. But what? Maybe he could grab the pen from Dad's hand, jump up on the sofa and drive it, hard, into Vincent's face? But the man was a trained killer and would surely be expecting something like that.

It would be madness to make a move now. So what else could he—?

Everybody jumped at a loud *crash* from just outside the lodge, the sound of glass shattering under a powerful impact. Vincent took a step back from the sofa, slipped the knife into his belt and swung the gun round towards the door. The Fixer stood up from his chair, a fearful expression on his face. 'What the hell was that?' he snapped.

'Search me.' Vincent pulled a pistol from a holster at his waist. He came round the side of the sofa and handed it to the Fixer. 'Watch them,' he hissed, nodding at the captives. The Fixer frowned, but he did as he was told, training the weapon on them while Vincent hurried back towards the door, the shotgun held ready to fire. He went to the little panel of glass in the door and peered cautiously through it. Then he reached out a hand and flicked on the porch light. He swore under his breath.

'What is it?' asked the Fixer.

'Your car,' said Vincent, and the Fixer started to move, but Vincent waved him back to his position. He unlatched the door and swung it open, looking cautiously outside. Through the open doorway, Jack caught a glimpse of the Fixer's car, a black Mercedes, illuminated by the porch light. Somebody had picked up the heavy stone statue of a lion that stood beside the front door and thrown it at the car's windscreen, smashing a great jagged hole in it. The lion's head was framed in a crazed circle of glass, snarling silently out from the devastation.

And a thought flashed through Jack's mind then. No ordinary man would have the strength to pick up that statue and throw it!

The Fixer had moved to one side so he could also look out of the door. He saw what had happened and gave a low groan. 'What the hell is going on here?' he snapped, but Vincent ignored him. He ducked outside and was gone for a few moments, his footsteps crunching back and forth on the gravel, as he checked all available hiding places. After a little while, he came back inside and closed the door after him. He glared at Jack.

'Who else is out there?' he demanded.

'I don't know,' said Jack.

'There must be somebody!' snarled Vincent. 'Is there someone working with you? There has to be!'

'It could be my dad,' said Rhona.

Vincent looked at her. 'Your *dad*?' he muttered.

'Maybe he came looking for me and worked out what

was happening. He has a shotgun, by the way, and he knows how to use it.'

'How would he know anything? The curtains are drawn, he couldn't see into the house. And why would he smash up a stranger's car?'

'Maybe he doesn't like posh cars,' Rhona told him and she smiled sweetly at the Fixer. Vincent glared at her, as though considering punching her.

'And he's built like Superman, is he, your dad? Strong enough to pick up a stone statue and throw it?'

'Maybe,' said Rhona. 'When he's in a mood.'

'How am I supposed to get back to London?' asked the Fixer.

Vincent looked at him. 'You'll have to take the other car,' he said. He nodded at Dad. '*His* car.'

The Fixer grimaced as though the thought of driving Dad's red hatchback was the worst thing he could imagine.

Vincent seemed to be thinking furiously. He looked at the Fixer. 'OK, before you do anything else, you need to bring my vehicle up here,' he said. He pulled a set of car keys from his pocket. 'It's a black Range Rover, it's parked thirty yards up the main road. Turn right at the top of the drive.' He threw the keys to the Fixer who caught them in his left hand.

'Maybe I should take *your* car,' reasoned the Fixer. 'Get the hell out of here and call in reinforcements.'

'We don't need 'em,' said Vincent, but he didn't sound very convincing. 'Look, just fetch my vehicle, OK? All my equipment's in the back. The stuff I need to . . .' He gestured quickly around. 'You know,' he added. 'Bring it here and then you can take the other one.'

'I'm not your errand boy,' snapped the Fixer.

'I'm aware of that,' said Vincent. 'But my associate isn't here, is he? He's gone missing. And I need what's in the Range Rover.'

'You expect me to go outside with some maniac lurking in the bushes?' cried the Fixer. 'What if he decides to put that statue into my skull next time?'

'You've got a gun,' reasoned Vincent. 'Anyone comes at you, just let them have it. There's fifteen bullets in the clip.'

'I usually leave this kind of thing to the hired muscle.'

Vincent sneered. 'You know how to pull a trigger, don't you? Point blank range, you can't miss. You'll be fine. Go and get the Range Rover. It'll take you five minutes, tops. Just bring it here and park it out front. And while you're gone, I'll get Sonny Jim here to sign those papers for you. Then you can be on your way.'

The Fixer looked far from convinced. 'I don't like this,' he muttered. 'Who the hell did that to my car?'

'Maybe . . . maybe it was Philbert?' murmured Jack. It was more of a question than a statement, but he was beginning to feel a tiny spark of hope deep within him.

'Who the hell is Philbert?' snarled the Fixer.

'He's talking about a scarecrow,' said Rhona. 'Ignore him, he's off his meds.'

'Shut it, both of you,' suggested Vincent. 'Or so help me, I'll knock you into the middle of next week.' He nodded to the Fixer. 'The sooner you go, the sooner you'll be back,' he said.

'All right, but . . . I'll be having words about this when I get back to London. I've never seen such incompetence.'

'You do whatever you need to,' said Vincent. 'Just get moving.'

The Fixer looked angry, but he walked to the door and peered cautiously through the glass panel. He stood for a moment as though getting up his courage. He unlatched the door and leaned out, glancing quickly up and down the drive.

'It looks clear,' he murmured.

'Go then!' snapped Vincent. 'I'll cover you.'

The Fixer ducked out and hurried away. Vincent watched him for a moment and then pulled the door shut. He stood for an instant, as though considering his situation. Then he turned back to the others.

'Right,' he said. 'I'm sick of pussyfooting around.' He moved closer to the sofa, lifted the barrel of the shotgun and held the end of it against Dad's head. 'Sign the papers,' he said. 'Now. Or I'll sign 'em with your brains.'

Dad still had the file in his lap. He opened it with shaking hands, looking for the right place to sign. 'I . . . I'm not sure where to . . .'

'Sign it!' said Vincent and his voice was a cold as a fall of January snow. Dad finally found the right page. He uncapped the fountain pen and took a deep breath. He paused for a moment, looked at Jack, searchingly, as though seeking his approval. Jack nodded, realising that there really was nothing else Dad could do right now. 'Do it,' he whispered. Dad lifted the pen.

And then there was the sound of a gunshot outside. Then another, and another, followed by a silence so deep that Jack thought he could hear his own heart beating in his chest.

CHAPTER TWENTY-ONE
A VISITOR

Jack looked at Vincent, who was still standing by the front door, peering out through the little window. The Fixer had been gone for something like twenty minutes now.

'I really don't think he's coming back,' said Jack, cautiously.

Vincent gave him a fierce glare. 'When I want your opinion, I'll ask for it,' he said, but it was clear he was badly rattled by the Fixer's non-return. His mask of authority was beginning to slip and he seemed dangerously close to panicking.

'You said yourself, it would only take him five minutes to get the car,' Jack reminded him. 'So where is he?'

'You heard the gun,' snarled Vincent. 'Three shots. Whoever came at him must be dead. Even *he* couldn't miss at close range.'

'You reckon?' Jack was beginning to feel another stirring

of hope. Could it be that Philbert had been bluffing back there in the field? Had he somehow managed to untie himself from the cross and come across to the lodge to try and help? The fact that Rhona was being held hostage would be a strong incentive. He was dedicated to protecting her . . . Jack shook his head, telling himself not to get his hopes up. Maybe he was just kidding himself. Maybe there was some other explanation.

He realised that Vincent was glaring at him. He looked angry enough to use that shotgun on him right now, but something must be telling him to hold off, maybe the thought that he might need a hostage himself.

Vincent transferred his gaze to Dad, who was still sitting there with the file on his lap. 'Have you signed that bloody thing yet?' he wanted to know.

Dad shook his head. 'I dropped the pen when the gun fired,' he said. 'I think it went down the side of the sofa.'

'Oh, for Christ's sake!' Vincent started pacing up and down again. He looked frantic, Jack thought, close to breaking point. 'Where *is* he?' he murmured. 'What's he playing at?' He stopped pacing as an unexpected sound came from the back of the house; what sounded like somebody knocking loudly on the kitchen door. Vincent stood for a moment, looking as though he might be about to panic – but then he waved the shotgun at his prisoners. 'Right, I want everybody upstairs!' he barked. '*Now*! Anybody tries something stupid and I promise you I will shoot. Go!'

Jack helped Dad get to his feet and Rhona jumped up out of the armchair. Jack led the way to the staircase and pushed Dad ahead of him. They went up the stairs in a tight cluster, horribly aware that Vincent was coming up close behind them, prodding at them with the shotgun. 'Turn right!' he shouted, and Dad turned right into the front bedroom.

Downstairs, there came another knock on the back door, louder this time, as though whoever was out there was getting impatient. Vincent hesitated by the bedroom door, looking anxiously down the staircase. Jack went instinctively to the window and stared out across the moonlit cornfield. He felt a powerful wave of disappointment jolt through him. Philbert was in his customary position, arms outstretched, hat pulled down low over his face . . . so who could that be, knocking on the door? Had somebody alerted the police? Was a rescue close at hand? But what policeman would have the strength to pick up that stone lion? Jack turned away from the window, more confused than ever.

Vincent came into the room looking like he meant business. He grabbed Dad and pushed him roughly down onto the floor, his back up against one end of an old-fashioned cast-iron radiator. Vincent propped the shotgun against the wall, reached into his pocket and pulled out a cable tie. Then he started to force Dad's hands behind his back.

'No!' Dad tried to resist and Vincent fetched him a clout across the side of his face, which slammed his head back against the radiator. Jack reacted instinctively, tried to go to his dad's defence, but another punch from Vincent sent him reeling backwards to slump down in a corner of the room. Now Rhona made a move towards the shotgun and she too received a punch that sent her sprawling to the floor. By the time Jack's head was clear, Dad was tied to the radiator, his head slumped forward.

Vincent beckoned to Rhona. 'Come 'ere,' he said and she shook her head, tears rolling down her cheeks. 'I mean it,' he added. 'Or do you want this?' He grabbed the gun and gestured with it. She got to her feet, and went reluctantly over to him. He pulled out yet another cable tie and tethered her at the other end of the radiator, securing her hands behind her back. He spent a bit of time checking that he was happy with both sets of bonds and then he looked at Jack. 'Right,' he said. 'Let's get this sorted. You're coming with me.' He picked up the shotgun, grabbed Jack by the lapels of his jacket and pulled him upright.

Jack was too dazed to resist as Vincent pushed him out of the room and back down the staircase. 'Into the kitchen,' Vincent told him, and Jack had no option but to do as he was told. As he stepped through the doorway, he saw that Douglas's precious gun cabinet was hanging open, the lock smashed, and he realised that Vincent must have broken it open in order to get the shotgun he was carrying. Through the half open door, Jack could see that the other gun was still in its mount, together with what looked like a couple of boxes of shells. He told himself that if he could just get hold of the weapon, maybe he could turn the tables . . .

'Don't even think about it,' said Vincent, clearly guessing Jack's intentions. He gave Jack a push towards the back door. 'I want you to open it,' he murmured. Jack stumbled closer and tried the handle. It was locked, but the key was in place, so he turned it, then twisted the handle again and pulled the door open. 'Step outside,' instructed Vincent.

Jack did as he was told and found himself standing in the dark back garden. Vincent came straight after him, the shotgun held ready to fire at anybody who might be standing there. He stood for a moment, looking around. 'Show yourself,' he barked. 'Try anything funny and I'll shoot the kid.' He waited for a moment, but nobody spoke.

The garden appeared to be deserted. The row of trees and shrubs that marked its border swayed restlessly in the wind. Vincent muttered something under his breath, looking this way and that. Then he grabbed Jack by his shoulder and pushed him ahead of him. 'Go round the side of the house,' he said. 'Slowly.' He prodded Jack in the small of the back with the gun and once again, Jack could only do as he was told. He realised what Vincent was doing: using him as a human shield. He snatched in a deep breath and then began to walk.

They moved round the side of the lodge, but there was nothing to be seen here, just a narrow border of flowerbeds to their left. They came to the front of the house, where the two vehicles were parked. The porch light was still on and the stone lion's head scowled from the shattered remains of the Fixer's windscreen. There was no sign of anybody. 'Where the hell is he?' hissed Vincent.

'Maybe he ran out on you,' said Jack. 'Maybe he took your Range Rover and headed back to London.'

'He wouldn't do that,' murmured Vincent – but he didn't sound very sure of himself. 'And anyway, what about those shots we heard? Who was he firing at?'

Just then, a vehicle turned on to the drive off the main road, its headlights blazing. Vincent grabbed Jack and pulled him back into cover. Jack felt a sudden surge of hope, telling himself that this might be a police car, come to investigate the sound of those gunshots, but hope was almost instantly replaced by anger when he recognised the approaching vehicle, a dark blue BMW.

The car pulled to a halt, the lights clicked off and the driver sat behind the wheel for a few moments, staring at the lodge. Then the driver's door opened and Douglas got out, looking warily around. He reacted when Vincent pushed Jack ahead of him, into the glow of the porch light. Douglas looked surprised for an instant and then very, very guilty. He took in the shattered windscreen of the Fixer's car and his eyes widened in surprise. 'What the hell's going on here?' he asked.

'That's a very good question,' snarled Vincent. 'You took your time getting back, didn't ya?'

'I was miles away when you rang,' said Douglas. 'It was the last thing I expected. Giles told me I wouldn't have to be here for any of this.' He couldn't seem to look Jack in the eye. 'What are you doing standing out here?'

'Trying to find out who's been playing silly beggars,' said Vincent.

'What do you mean?'

'Frank's disappeared and so has Pemberton.' Jack noticed he was too flustered now to remember not to mention people's real names. 'I sent him out to get my Range Rover half an hour ago and there was gunshots. There's been no sign of him since. Then, a few minutes ago, some joker started knocking on the back door.'

'What? Who could that have been?'

'If I knew that, I wouldn't be standing out here like an idiot, would I?' Vincent shook his head. 'This is all going to hell in a handcart,' he said. 'And I reckon this kid knows more than he's letting on. I think there's somebody helping him.'

Douglas finally got the courage to look at Jack. 'Jack, if you know something, you'd really be well advised to tell us about it,' he said.

Jack sneered. He felt suddenly more confident, his anger rising within him like molten steel. 'You scumbag,' he said. 'I'm amazed you had the nerve to show your face back here, after what you've done.'

Douglas didn't reply to that. He looked at Vincent. 'Did you . . . did you at least get the papers signed?'

'No, not yet.'

'Well, we need to get it sorted, before . . .' Douglas didn't seem able to continue with that.

'I know. I thought you might like to help persuade your old mate to sign.'

Douglas shook his head. 'Oh no, I . . . I can't,' he said.

Vincent chuckled. 'What's the matter?' he asked. 'Not able to look him in the eye? You're not exactly the hard man, are you?'

'You know perfectly well, it's not my line of work. I'm a—'

'A rat, that's what you are, pal. I've worked with some creeps in my time, but you take the bleeding biscuit.' Vincent shook his head and spat a big glob of phlegm on the ground, inches from Douglas's Nikes. 'All right,' he said, 'since you're so *sensitive*, I suppose I'll have to do it.' He handed Douglas the shotgun. 'I hope you know how to use one of these,' he said.

'I ought to. It's my gun. How did you get hold of it?'

'How d'yer think? Had to break open the cupboard, didn't I?'

'I don't recall giving you permission to handle my stuff.'

Vincent shrugged his shoulders. 'Special circumstances,' he said. He nodded at the gun. 'So . . . you've got some experience with that thing?'

'I've killed pheasants,' said Douglas. 'And grouse.'

'There's no real difference. These are just bigger targets, that's all. Easier to hit. You guard Sonny Jim here, while I'm gone. Make sure he doesn't make a run for it. If he tries, shoot him.'

'Seriously?'

'I never joke about things like that. Just blow a hole through him. I'll go back in and see about sorting out that signature. Once that's done, we'll go together to get the stuff from my Range Rover.'

'What *stuff*?' asked Douglas.

'The equipment I need to rig the fire.'

'Oh I . . . I really don't . . .'

Vincent looked intently at Douglas and then shook his head again. 'Don't try and look all innocent, sunshine, cos I happen to know that it was your idea in the first place.'

'No, I—'

'Sure it was! Leave no evidence, you said.' He jerked a

thumb over his shoulder. 'And I suppose you've got the place insured, so it's not like you'll lose anything, is it?'

'I didn't . . . I never said . . .' Douglas's face was bright red with shame. Jack turned to look at him and Vincent sniggered.

'Yeah, that's right,' he told Jack, seemingly delighted by Douglas's discomfort. 'Your old man's best mate. He didn't just sell him out. He came up with the plan as well. Oh, he's a right charmer, this one. It's always the posh boys you have to watch out for.' He turned away, laughing unpleasantly. 'I'll leave you two to have a little chat,' he said, and strode back around the side of the house. Jack continued to stare at Douglas in undisguised hatred.

'Your idea,' he murmured. 'You're going to burn down the lodge with us inside?'

'Oh, you . . . you don't want to believe what *he* says,' stammered Douglas. 'He'd tell you anything. I . . . I was assured that you and your dad wouldn't be harmed. They . . . they promised me that much. In fact, I insisted on it. And that . . . that was a lie about the fire, by the way. It's the first I've heard of it.'

Jack gazed at him for a moment. 'Honestly?' he murmured.

'Yes, absolutely.'

'All right, then. Let's go, shall we?'

Douglas looked at him in surprise. 'Go?' he murmured.

'Yeah, we'll get in your car and we'll go and find the police, tell them what's happening here. Since you don't want anybody to be harmed.'

There was a long silence. Then Douglas shook his head. 'I . . . can't do that, Jack,' he said quietly. 'I'm in too deep.'

'All right, then,' said Jack. '*I'll* go.'

Douglas narrowed his eyes. 'You?' he murmured.

'Sure. When Vincent comes back, just tell him I got away from you. I'll go and find some help.' He started to walk away along the drive but froze in his tracks at the sound of a harsh metallic click behind him. He turned back slowly to see that Douglas had cocked the gun and was aiming it at his chest.

'Stay where you are,' he warned.

'Or what?' asked Jack.

'Or I'll . . . just stay where you are, please . . .'

'Say it!' yelled Jack.

'I . . . I'm sorry but . . .'

'SAY IT!'

'Or I'll pull the trigger,' snapped Douglas.

And that was when Jack let Douglas have it. He called him every filthy name he could think of, yelling each of them as loudly as he could, his voice echoing in the night. Douglas just stood there and took it, his face expressionless, but his eyes filled with tears, which at least gave Jack a little satisfaction. When he'd finally run out of swear words, he felt better. He tried not to think about what was coming – how he and Dad and poor Rhona would be left in the cottage for dead, while the place burned down around them.

'How much?' he asked quietly.

Douglas looked at him and Jack could see that now the tears were trickling down his face. 'I'm sorry?' Douglas whispered.

'How much are they paying you for this?'

Douglas shook his head. 'You . . . you have to understand, Jack. I was desperate. The gambling, you see. I'd racked up these massive debts that I couldn't pay back, not in a hundred years. They were going to take my apartment in London, my car . . . I was going to lose my job! This was my one chance for salvation. I had to take it. You . . . you can see that, can't you? I really didn't have any choice!'

Jack frowned. 'How much?' he asked again.

Douglas stared at him.

'I don't understand,' he murmured.

'How much are they paying you for this? I need to know.'

Douglas looked down at his feet. 'A million,' he said quietly.

'So that's what three people's lives are worth, is it?' observed Jack. 'A million pounds. Well, I hope it was worth it.'

Douglas had no answer for that one. He lifted his head and looked curiously towards the side of the house. 'What's taking Vincent so long?' he wondered aloud. 'He said he was just going in to get the papers signed.'

Jack shrugged. 'Perhaps he can't find the pen,' he said. 'Or . . .' An idea occurred to him. 'Or perhaps somebody got to him.'

Douglas scowled. 'What do you mean?' he murmured.

Jack shrugged. 'Well, he *has* been gone quite a while,' he said. 'And there's been somebody sneaking around all night.' He pointed to the Fixer's car. 'Somebody did that. Just picked up the statue and threw it. I mean, look at that thing! It would have to be somebody very strong to do that. Well, I couldn't lift it. Could you? And then, later on, there was somebody knocking at the back door . . . that's why we were out here when you arrived. Your mate was trying to find out who it was.'

Douglas looked uncomfortable. 'He's no mate of mine,' he said quietly. 'Look, if you know something, Jack . . . if there really is somebody helping you, you'd better tell me about it.'

Jack looked at him. 'Your guess is as good as mine,' he said.

Douglas gestured with the barrel of the gun. 'We'll go back round to the kitchen,' he said. 'Slowly. And I need you to keep your hands where I can see them.'

Jack sighed. He was getting very tired of being ordered about, but right now, he didn't see that he had any other option but to obey; so he started walking, his hands raised above his head. He and Douglas went round the side of the lodge and into the back garden. The trees were still swaying restlessly in the wind, but it was something else that suddenly caught Jack's attention – something that was hanging from one of the trees. He stopped walking and stood there, staring open-mouthed. Douglas came to a halt too and they examined the thing in the tree. It was the body of a man, hanging upside down, his feet jammed into the fork of a low branch, his arms behind his back. An old rag had been tied tightly across his mouth and his eyes were closed. A thick trickle of blood oozed down his face from a deep gash in his forehead. Jack could see that his chest was rising and falling, but it was evident at a glance that he was out cold.

CHAPTER TWENTY-TWO
FIGHT OR FLIGHT

'Oh . . . my . . . God!' Douglas was staring at Vincent in absolute terror, the shotgun, for the moment, pointing at the ground. He glanced at Jack. 'Who . . . who could have done this?' he gasped.

'It has to be Philbert,' said Jack, with a calmness that surprised him. 'I really don't see how it can be anybody else.'

Douglas glared at him. 'What are you talking about? Philbert? The scarecrow? How could *he* have anything to do with this? You really do need to take your meds, boy.'

Jack shrugged. 'I know it sounds crazy. But he's more than just a scarecrow.'

'Don't be . . . ridiculous! That's crazy talk!'

Jack nodded. 'Yeah, I suppose it is,' he admitted. 'And maybe that's it. Maybe I've gone crazy. Maybe all this –' he waved his hands around him – 'is some kind of . . .

hallucination. Maybe I'll wake up in a minute and it will all have been some horrible dream.' He waved a hand at Vincent's limp figure. 'But think about it for a minute. Somebody lifted him up into that tree. You'd have to be very big and strong to do that. Stronger than a man.'

Douglas looked desperately around. He was clearly on the very edge of panic, visibly shaking and breathing erratically. It occurred to Jack that perhaps this was his one chance to try and grab that shotgun but the instant he started to make his move, Douglas came abruptly to his senses and snapped the weapon back up to point it at Jack's chest. 'What are you doing?' Douglas gasped.

'I'm just trying to . . .'

'We'll go back to my car,' snapped Douglas. He waved the gun. 'Yes, that's what we'll do. Right now. We're going to the car . . . and we're getting out of here.'

Jack gave him a disbelieving look. 'Really?' He waved a hand at Vincent. 'What about your friend?'

'He's no friend of mine,' snarled Douglas.

'But we can't just leave.'

'Watch me!'

'What if I say I'm not going with you? What if I say I want to stay here with my Dad and—'

Jack broke off with a yell as Douglas stepped forward and slapped him hard across the face, nearly knocking him to the ground. Before he quite knew what was happening, Douglas had him by his collar and was frogmarching him back round the side of the lodge to the BMW, clearly intent on keeping Jack as a hostage. He wrenched open the passenger door and threw Jack down into the seat, then slammed the door on him. Douglas got in behind the wheel, keeping the shotgun propped up beside him. He started the engine, threw the car into reverse and they shot wildly backwards along the drive.

Once they reached the main road, Douglas brought the car round in a screeching half circle, put it into first gear and started driving. Jack looked hopefully towards the field, expecting to see Philbert's cross standing empty in its midst – but no, he could see, quite clearly in the moonlight, that Philbert was still in his usual position, arms outstretched, face staring straight ahead. So who had ambushed Vincent?

Then Douglas stamped down on the pedal and the car accelerated away.

Realising he had to do something, Jack made a frantic grab for the steering wheel, but Douglas punched him hard, rocking him back against the passenger window. Lights seemed to explode momentarily in front of Jack's eyes and he was aware of warm blood trickling from his nose. Only now did Douglas think to switch on the car's headlights, throwing two beams of brilliant white light lancing along the road ahead of them.

And suddenly, incredibly, Philbert was there, standing right in the middle of the road, his arms outstretched, glaring angrily back into the headlights, his eyes reflecting the light back at the car. He was walking straight towards the oncoming vehicle as though determined to collide with it. Douglas yelled something that Jack didn't quite catch and Jack lunged again, wrenched the steering wheel over to the right, desperately trying to swerve around Philbert's hulking figure. There was a squeal of brakes, the tyres shredding on the rough surface of the tarmac. The BMW seemed to take off into thin air. It breasted the ditch at the side of the road and the broad trunk of an oak tree came lurching towards them. The front bumper slammed into it, the impact rocking the car, and Jack's world was suddenly obliterated by a huge white balloon that blossomed in front of him and smacked him in the face, like a punch from a giant's fist. Blackness rippled through him.

For a few moments, he knew nothing. He drifted in a

limbo of booming sound and then, quite suddenly, came back to his senses. The airbag was slowly deflating in front of him and he was dimly aware that Douglas was in motion beside him, throwing open the driver's door and flailing out of the vehicle, cursing as he went. There was an over-powering stink of petrol and warm liquid sprayed across Jack's legs. He willed himself to move, but for a few moments, he couldn't seem to get control of his limbs. He felt like a puppet with severed strings and he had to shake his head to clear it of the fog that was threatening to engulf him. He finally managed to fumble open the door, though it took considerable effort, and he half jumped, half fell out of the car and down into the ditch. Icy water flooded his trainers, rising up to his ankles, the shock waking him up a little. With an effort, he brought his eyes back into focus. He saw that there was a field on the far side of the ditch, another hayfield, this one bordered by trees, and then he noticed that Douglas was trudging through the waist-high grass, still clutching the shotgun in one hand. Beyond him, the sky was finally turning to morning in a tumbled splendour of red cloud.

For a moment, Jack thought about running straight back to the lodge, but the idea that Douglas might escape made him fearless. He managed to scramble up through a gap in the hedge and into the field, though his limbs seemed to belong to somebody else. Douglas too was walking like a drunken man, swaying from side to side, stumbling as the long dry stalks of grass snatched at his petrol-soaked legs. Jack followed him, realising as he went that he was pretty much unhurt by the collision, except for a dull ache in his neck, doubtless caused by the impact of the airbag. He quickened his pace until he was just a few metres behind Douglas.

'Hey,' he said. 'Hey, you! Wait!'

Douglas reeled round, bringing the shotgun up to a firing position. Jack saw that he had a deep gash over one eye from which a stream of dark blood pumped. 'Go back,' he said wearily. 'Get lost.'

'Where do you think you're going?' Jack asked him.

'I don't know,' said Douglas. 'Somewhere . . . somewhere else.' He coughed, spat out a couple of broken teeth, wiped his mouth on his sleeve. 'On the road . . . I thought I saw . . .' He shook his head, not wanting to believe the evidence of his own eyes. 'It looked like . . .'

'Philbert,' said Jack. 'So you saw him too.'

Douglas looked puzzled as he tried to figure out the logic of that. 'What are you talking about?' he asked.

'It's not just me who can see him.'

Douglas laughed at that, a short bark of disbelief. 'You're crazy,' he said. 'Do you know that? You're absolutely—' He lifted his gaze to look over Jack's shoulder. 'Who the hell is *that*?' he asked suspiciously.

Jack turned to look. Philbert was coming through the hedge. He looked really strange because he wasn't wearing his hat and jacket. He was a tall, sinewy thing made of straw; but it was straw that seemed to pulse and ripple with incredible power.

'Christ,' said Douglas. 'Oh Jesus! What . . . what *is* that?'

'You *know* what it is,' said Jack, turning back. 'I've been trying to tell you.'

Douglas shook his head. 'But this . . . this isn't happening,' he cried. 'It's not . . . possible.'

'I'm afraid it is,' said Jack. 'I know how you feel, though. First time I saw it, I freaked! Listen, if I were you, I'd put the shotgun down. He really hates guns.'

Douglas was shaking his head, keeping the weapon trained on Philbert as he came steadily closer. The scarecrow was taking his time now, because there really was no need to hurry.

'You all right?' he asked Jack, as he came to stand beside him.

'I'm fine,' Jack assured him. 'What took you so long to come and help us?'

'Just waiting for the right moment,' said Philbert, matter-of-factly.

Jack nodded towards Douglas. 'What are you going to do to him?'

'That depends,' said Philbert. 'If he comes quietly, maybe I'll just . . . throw him around a bit. For fun. But somehow, I doubt that he *will* come quietly. His type never do.'

'Go easy on him,' said Jack. 'But . . . listen, there's something I don't understand. How did you . . .?'

'Later,' said Philbert. He started to walk towards Douglas.

'Stay back!' screamed Douglas. 'Stay back or I'll shoot!'

Philbert kept walking.

'I'm warning you! I'll pull the trigger!'

Jack frowned, turning away. He began to walk back towards the hedge, because he really didn't want to see what happened next.

'No!' he heard Douglas yell. 'No, STOP!'

There was the sudden loud bang of the shotgun firing, a sound that stopped Jack in his tracks. He turned to see that Philbert now had a ragged hole blown clear through his chest and out of his back, through which Jack could see a blaze of orange sunlight. Philbert looked down at the damage in disbelief, then gave a bellow of pure rage and began to run at Douglas. Douglas dropped the gun and fumbled desperately in his pocket. He came out with something, something small and metallic that glinted in the gathering light and Jack knew instantly what it was.

The Zippo lighter.

'Oh no!' Jack began to run back towards the two figures, watching, horrified, as they slammed heavily into each other. Philbert's powerful arms wrapped around Douglas in a crushing embrace. Douglas screamed something unintelligible. There was a sudden flash of flame, which flared against Philbert's chest and flickered quickly upwards in a blaze of orange. In seconds, his upper torso was alight, but he kept his hold on Douglas, those powerful arms encircling him and the two of them fell sideways into the long grass. The flame exploded in a hideous eruption of yellow. Jack could feel the intense heat of it on his face as he stumbled to a halt and stood staring in horror at the conflagration that was taking place in the field, the sun-dried stalks of grass blackening and withering as the flames rippled outwards in a great wave. Jack caught a glimpse of two figures writhing in the midst of the heat. Then clouds of thick black smoke came rolling towards him, engulfing him, filling his eyes with tears and catching at the back of his throat, making him gasp for breath.

Reminding himself that his own clothes were soaked with petrol, Jack had no option but to retreat. He stumbled back through the grass to the hedge, clambered down through it and into the ditch, cringing once again as the cold water engulfed his feet. The BMW stood against the tree, smoke spilling from under its crumpled bonnet. Jack scrambled up the far side of the ditch and onto the road. He hesitated, peering hopefully back through the hedge, but the whole field was now alight and he knew instantly that there could be no hope for anything in its midst.

Jack stood for a minute, coughing the smoke out of his lungs, as he began to accept that there was nothing he could do. He started walking back towards the lodge, limping a little now as the pain of some of his minor injuries started to register and the tears in his eyes were nothing to do with the smoke he had inhaled. When he got to Philbert's field, he had a brief moment of hope, when he thought he saw the scarecrow still hanging on his cross – but when he paused and looked closer, he realised that it was actually Pemberton, the Fixer, dressed in the familiar hat and jacket, lashed into position with ropes, a cloth gag around his mouth, his eyes staring in silent rage at the boy on the road. And Jack finally understood how Philbert could appeared to have been in two places at the same time. Jack shook his head and, weeping, he ran on until he got to the lodge.

He went round the side of the building, noting as he did so that Vincent was still hanging, bound and gagged from the tree – and Jack wondered how he and Dad were ever going to explain away all the things that had happened here. He went in through the open back door. As he slowly climbed the stairs to the front bedroom, he was already running through what he would say to Dad and Rhona when he finally got to them – how much he would tell them and how much he thought they would actually believe.

EPILOGUE

On the way over to the farm, Dad spotted Ken's Land Rover parked beside Philbert's field. Ken was working on the catch of the gate, which had somehow been damaged and Jack saw that Rhona was standing in the midst of the corn, working on a new scarecrow. A line of crows watched resentfully from the wall. Dad pulled up behind the Land Rover and wound the window down. Ken left what he was doing and wandered over to talk. 'So you're on your way home then?' he said.

Dad nodded. Both his and Jack's faces still carried the bruises of the various punches they'd recently suffered. To Jack, the last forty-eight hours had passed in a blur. When he'd finally untied Dad and Rhona, she had run to the farm to summon help. The ambulance that arrived a short time later had taken Jack and Dad to the nearest hospital and, of course, while they were there they'd spoken at great length to the police, though there'd been precious little of any use they could tell them.

Yes, three strangers had turned up at the lodge in the middle of the night and taken them hostage. No, they had no idea who had attacked the strangers and tied them up. It had all happened while they were imprisoned inside. One man was found, bound and gagged, hanging from a tree in the back garden. A second was tied to a cross in the field where the McFarlanes' old scarecrow used to be. And a short search in the woods had turned up a third man, the one they only knew as 'Frank'. Like his companions, he had been knocked unconscious and securely tied, and when questioned by the police, would only say that he had been jumped by an unseen assailant. All three men were currently refusing to name the individual who had paid them to do the job, but the police were confident that one of them would confess before too long.

And then there was the fourth man, the one that Dad *did* know, his former friend Douglas. He had crashed his BMW into the ditch whilst trying to flee the scene and had abandoned it. His charred corpse had been found in a burnt-out hayfield, a short distance from the lodge, a Zippo lighter still clutched in his blackened hand.

Dad had done what he really should have done in the first place. He told the police everything he knew about the people on that list he'd made – and he had given the names of those whom he suspected had sent the bad guys after him.

Jack and Dad had finally been told that it was OK for them to return to London. They would be met on arrival, however, by members of the Metropolitan Police, who would be keeping a very close eye on them until all this went to trial.

'I'm so sorry,' Dad told Ken, as he leaned in at the window of the car. 'If I'd had any idea that Rhona might get mixed up in any of this, I'd never have come to the lodge in the first place.'

Ken smiled, shrugging his broad shoulders. 'How could you have known?' he asked. 'Your best friend sold you out. Nobody could have seen that coming. Terrible what happened to him, though. Have the police any idea why he set fire to my neighbour's field?'

Dad shook his head. 'They're working on the theory that he had some kind of accident when he was driving away. Probably got petrol on his clothes in the crash. Maybe he stopped to have a cigarette and . . . boom! I did try telling him that they were bad for his health.' He glanced at Jack. 'Thank God he decided to leave Jack behind when he left the vehicle.'

'And what about the other stuff?' asked Ken. 'Who attacked the bad guys? Do they have any theories?'

Dad shook his head. 'They're as bewildered as we are. Obviously, *somebody* was trying to help us, but we'll probably never know who it was – all we do know is that somebody smashed up that man's car, somebody attacked those guys one by one and tied them up . . . and somebody was hammering on the back door – I mean, we didn't imagine any of that, did we?'

'That statue must have weighed a ton,' said Ken. 'Who the hell would have the strength to pick that up and throw it? Whoever it was must have been very powerful.' He shook his head. 'And then the daftest thing of all. What did they do with *Philbert*?'

Jack opened the passenger door. 'I'll go and say goodbye to Rhona,' he suggested, and the two men smiled and nodded.

He got out of the car and walked through the corn to Rhona. He saw that she had the scarecrow pretty much put together now, the old clothes stuffed tight with straw.

She had lifted him into position against the wooden stake and was lashing him onto the crossbar.

'Hey,' he said.

She turned to look at him. 'Hey,' she said back. 'You all set?'

He nodded.

She studied his battered face for a few moments. 'You look a fright,' she said, and then grinned, to show that she didn't really mean it.

'You can't talk,' he told her, indicating a purple bruise on her left jaw.

She smiled sadly. 'I suppose once you're away back to London, you'll forget all about me.'

'No way,' he said. 'Are you kidding? I'll send you a friend request as soon as I get home to my phone. What about yours?'

'Oh, luckily I had insurance. I've already ordered a new one.' She smiled. 'Online,' she added, just to drive home the point. 'Because that's how we roll out here in the country.'

He grinned, acknowledging the dig. 'Good,' he said. 'We'll be able to message each other. And you're coming to visit, right? I'll take you shopping in the big city. Show you all the sights.'

'We'll see,' she said. 'I doubt you'll give me a thought, once you're home.'

'Don't count on it,' he told her.

She turned back to the scarecrow, finished buttoning up his jacket.

'That's not bad,' observed Jack. 'Your mum would be proud of you.'

'It's not Philbert, though,' said Rhona, sadly. 'It's not the one she made.' She took a step back and studied her efforts thoughtfully. 'Why would they have *done* such a thing?' she wondered aloud. 'Stealing a scarecrow? It doesn't make sense. In all the panic of somebody attacking them, why would they decide to do that?'

'Maybe they wanted his clothes to use as a disguise,' suggested Jack. 'Maybe that's why one of them was wearing his hat and jacket? The rest of him . . . well, they could have just . . . torn him up and . . . scattered him, I guess.' He waved a hand at the surrounding corn.

Rhona looked around but she seemed far from convinced.

'Jack, what you were saying before,' she murmured. 'About Philbert being able to talk . . . and move?'

Jack studied his feet for a moment. 'I'm back on my meds now,' he told her, and for once, he was actually telling the truth. He'd decided to take them as prescribed from now on. It seemed to make sense. And besides, he didn't have to wonder about Philbert any more. Because, in those final moments before the fire, Douglas had seen him too . . .

'I'm glad you're being sensible,' said Rhona. 'It makes me feel happier, to know you're looking after yourself.' She turned to face him and smiled. 'Well then, I hope you have a nice trip back. I'll . . . miss you.' They looked at each other for quite a while, unsure of how to handle this, but it was Jack who finally made the first move. He stepped closer, put his arms round her and held her against him. As he did, he looked over her shoulder at the new scarecrow. Rhona had found an old Guy Fawkes mask from somewhere and the face that stared back at him was totally devoid of life. He felt a twinge of sadness go through him, thinking that he would have loved the chance to talk to Philbert one more time. To thank him for what he'd done. He released Rhona and stepped back, now more than ever realising that he wanted to see her again . . . that he *needed* to, before very much longer.

'Well,' he said. 'I'd er . . . better let you get back to work.'

She smiled at him. 'Who will I have to talk to now you're gone?' she murmured.

'Talk to *him*,' he said, nodding to the scarecrow 'He looks like a good listener. What are you going to call him, by the way?'

She thought for a moment. 'Jack,' she said. 'I'm going to name him after you.'

He laughed at that. 'Well, look after each other,' he said. 'And you'll definitely be hearing from me. I promise.' He turned and walked back to the car. Just before he got in, he looked across the field at Rhona. She was standing beside the new scarecrow. From this distance, they made an odd couple, he thought, she leaning against him, he with one arm apparently stretched across her shoulders. Jack waved and she waved back. He opened the door and climbed into the passenger seat. Dad and Ken were exchanging a last few words.

'Well,' said Ken. 'Don't forget now, if you're ever back this way . . .'

'We'll call in,' said Dad. 'Of course we will.' He glanced at his son. 'Something tells me we'll be back here before very much longer. And thanks for being so understanding, Ken. I really don't think I deserve it.' He turned to look at Jack. 'You ready to go?' he asked.

'As I'll ever be,' said Jack. 'And, Dad, remember, from now on. No more secrets, OK?'

Dad smiled ruefully. 'Don't worry,' he said. 'I've learned my lesson.' He started the engine and looked across the field at Rhona and the scarecrow. 'That isn't much of an improvement on the last one,' he muttered. 'Still as ugly as sin.'

'Careful,' Jack advised him. 'You don't want to hurt his feelings, do you?'

'Ken's feelings?' muttered Dad.

'No, Jack's. The new scarecrow. That's his name.'

Dad shook his head. 'You're as crazy as they are,' he concluded.

He put the car into gear and they drove slowly away, but Jack turned in his seat and kept watching over his shoulder, until Rhona and the scarecrow were finally lost from sight.

THE PIPER

Winner of the Scottish Children's Book Award

DANNY WESTON

He who pays the piper calls the tune

On the eve of World War Two, Peter and Daisy are evacuated to a remote farmhouse. From the moment they arrive, they are aware that something evil haunts the place. Who plays the eerie music that can only be heard at night? And why is Daisy so irresistibly drawn to it? When Peter uncovers a dark family secret, he begins to realise that his sister is in terrible danger, and to save her he must face an ancient curse…

'Wonderfully twisty chiller that's sure to make you want to keep all of the lights on'
Scotsman

9781783440511 £7.99